SKATING

IN THE

DARK

SKATING

IN THE

DARK

DAVID MICHAEL KAPLAN

PANTHEON BOOKS

NEW YORK

The following chapters have been previously published, in slightly
different form: "Stand" in the *Atlantic;* "Homecoming" (as
"Unfinished Business") in *Redbook;* "Piano Lessons" in
American Short Fiction; "Feral Cats" in *Story Magazine;* and "In the
Night" in the *Indiana Review.* "Stand" was reprinted
in *O. Henry Prize Stories 1990.*

"Piano Lessons" and "Camel" were PEN Syndicated Fiction Project
prizewinners. "Piano Lessons" was also produced on
National Public Radio's "Sound of Writing" series.

Grateful acknowledgment is made to the following for
permission to reprint previously published material:
Penguin USA: "Summer People" originally appeared
in much different form in *Comfort* by David Michael Kaplan.
Copyright © 1987 by David Michael Kaplan. Reprinted by permission
of Viking Penguin, a division of Penguin Books USA Inc.
Clockus Music, Inc.: Excerpt from the song lyrics "Do You
Want To Dance?" by Bobby Freeman. Copyright © 1958 by
Clockus Music, Inc. Reprinted by permission.

Library of Congress Cataloging-in-Publication Data
Kaplan, David Michael.
Skating in the dark / David Michael Kaplan.
p.   cm.
ISBN 0-679-40517-8
I. Title.
PS3561.A5537S57   1991
813'.54—dc20   91-8365

Book Design by Chris Welch
Manufactured in the United States of America
First Edition

To Joyce,
and to the memory of my mother

Instead of the swift and imperceptible flowing of time, you are aware of its nodes, those points where time stands still or from which it leaps ahead. And you slip into the breaks and look around.

Ralph Ellison, *Invisible Man*

Shall I say it again? In order to arrive there,
To arrive where you are, to get from where you are not,
You must go by a way wherein there is no ecstasy.

T. S. Eliot, *Four Quartets*

ACKNOWLEDGMENTS

The author is grateful to the National Endowment for the Arts, the Illinois Arts Council, the Pennsylvania Council on the Arts, the Yaddo Corporation, and Loyola University Chicago for their support during the writing of this novel.

Contents

Part III GHOSTS

Part IV HOMECOMING

Part I

ESCAPE

Piano Lessons

—December 1951

When *I was seven* years old, my mother decided I should have piano lessons. We had an old upright piano inherited from her uncle George on the side porch, and I think she felt it should be used. "Maybe Frank's musical," she told my father. "It'd be nice to hear music in the house." My father didn't like the idea at all. I'd never shown any interest in music, he said; it was a waste of time and money. (Money was on his mind a lot that fall and winter, since there was talk that the bearing plant where he was a line supervisor might close and relocate closer to Pittsburgh, and my father knew he would never leave Tyler, the little town in western Pennsylvania where we lived.) Most of all, though, he didn't like the idea of the nuns. Except for Mrs. Kresky, who lived thirty miles away in Schuylerville, the nuns at St. Stanislaus were the only piano teachers in

3

the county, let alone Tyler. "I don't like him being over there with them," my father said, but my mother was insistent.

"For God's sake," she told him, "what do you think they're going to do? Convert him?"

So on Wednesday afternoons that December, my father waited after school to take me to my piano lesson. As our Packard coughed and spluttered like an old, tired beast, we'd drive across the bridge to the Third Ward, the side of town where St. Stanislaus was. I'd crane my neck and look down at the frozen French River, its ice mottled and dirty. Once I asked my father where it went. "Nowhere," he said, and I thought, *The river is going nowhere.* We'd pass tired houses, their yards littered with broken toys, empty dog houses, rusted iceboxes and washers, cars slowly being stripped to skeletons. Often their lights weren't yet on, and I wondered if anybody really lived in those houses, and did they have children like me who also took piano lessons.

"Mind now," my father warned as he handed me a dollar for the lesson. "If those nuns try and teach you anything besides piano, you let me know."

I didn't know what he meant. I knew nothing about nuns, had never even been close to one until I started taking piano lessons, and his words frightened me.

"You just tell me," he said, "and we'll put an end to that. I don't care what your mother says." Then he'd leave me to go wait somewhere—I never knew where—while I had my lesson.

I'd knock on the priory door and be ushered into the small music room to wait for Sister Benedict. The room had a stale, waxy smell and was always too warm, the radiator hissing like a cornered cat. The drapes were kept closed, and shadows seemed everywhere. Above the piano, its finish worn away to a dull smoky brown, a wooden Christ gazed down on me in agony. Sometimes I'd hear doors softly opening and closing in the hallway, but I never saw any people pass by, or heard any voices or the sound of pianos being played by other children taking piano lessons. What I did hear was the rustle of Sister Benedict's habit in the hall, and then she'd be there, hands folded, lips thin and unsmiling, smelling like old sweaters and my mother's laundry starch. She'd nod and sit beside me on the piano bench, and uncover the keys. "Let's begin," she'd say.

I always played badly. Meter was a mystery to me. I was either going too fast or too slow, or losing the count altogether. "Do it again," Sister Benedict would murmur, and I would try, but still I couldn't get it right. Sometimes when I played particularly badly, she'd pinch the bridge of her nose between her fingers and rub. "Have you practiced?" she'd ask, and I'd nod, and she'd look at me, and purse her lips. "Again," she'd tell me, tapping her pencil on my music book in an attempt to mark the beat. I blinked with frustration as I struggled to find the proper rhythm. I rarely finished an exercise. "No, no—like this," Sister Benedict would interrupt, and then demonstrate. "Do you understand now?" I nodded, and tried to remember how she'd done it, but already it was slipping from my consciousness, it was still a mystery and a secret, and I didn't understand at all.

Later, my father would be waiting for me in the car, its motor running so he could keep warm: after the first lesson, he never went back inside the priory. "Did those nuns try and teach you anything?" he'd ask. "Besides piano?"

I shook my head.

"You let me know," he said.

At home my mother listened to me struggle practicing. "I think you're getting it," she'd say cheerfully.

"I haven't heard a tune yet," my father said.

And then one afternoon everything changed. Snow was falling thickly when my father dropped me off for my lesson. "I

have something for you," Sister Benedict said when she entered
the music room, and she was smiling, which she'd rarely done
before. She went to the closet and came back with something
I'd never seen, a wooden box with a metal shaft and scale. "I
got this for you," she said, putting the metronome on top of the
piano. "Maybe it will help." She wound it and pressed a button
on the side. The shaft clicked back and forth like an admonish-
ing finger. "Play," she told me. "Try keeping up." I tried, but
the metronome only made things worse. Like a shaming, clucking tongue, it seemed to mock me. My fingers stiffened. I
stopped playing.

Sister Benedict stopped the metronome. "What's the
matter?" she asked.

"I . . . I can't keep up."

"Let's try it slower," she said, and adjusted the metronome. But still I couldn't find the proper beat, and still the
metronome clicked back and forth, chiding me. I felt myself
sweating underneath my shirt.

Once more she reset it. "Try again," she urged.

But it was always gaining on me, pushing furiously on-
ward with a pace and a will of its own. Christ in his torment
looked down on me; Sister Benedict, eyes half-closed, listened
to me with a pained expression. My fingers missed more and
more notes, the page became a blur, and still the metronome
marched on, and with every tick and tock it seemed to say, *You
will do this again and again and again, you will never get it right,
you will never go home, you will be in this music room forever.*

My fingers froze. I began to cry.

"What's the matter?" Sister Benedict asked anxiously.
"Why are you crying?" I couldn't reply. I sat with my hands
rigidly by my side, chest heaving, my face hot with tears.

"Frank," she said, using my name for the first time.

"Please . . ." Her hand fluttered, as if she would touch me, then fell into her lap. "I don't understand," she said. "Please, stop crying." But I couldn't—I couldn't stop at all.

"Stay here," she murmured. And as much to herself as to me: "I'll get Mother Superior." She left and soon was back with an older nun, who wore a white shawl over her black habit. By then my sobs had quieted to short, choked hiccups.

"He just started bawling," Sister Benedict told her. "He won't stop."

"What's wrong, child?" the other nun gently asked. I shook my head. I couldn't say what was wrong.

"He has trouble," Sister Benedict said. "He gets frustrated easily."

The older nun put her hand on my forehead. "He feels hot." She stroked my hair. "He should go home early today."

"His father will be coming for him shortly," Sister Benedict said.

"Would you like to rest until your father comes?" the older nun asked me. I wiped my cheek and nodded. She took my hand and led me down the dark hallway to a narrow room with mullioned windows that looked out onto a courtyard lit by a single lamp on a post. Snow was still falling fast; it had already covered the bushes, the ground, the benches. I'd stopped crying now, but was still sniffling hard. "You can lie down over there until your father comes," the nun told me, pointing to a settee by the window. She softly closed the door.

Except for the ping of the radiator, the room was silent. I lay on the settee, hands folded on my chest. It seemed I could hear my heart beat, and, between beats, could feel my life slipping away, my future receding before it had even come to me, like the ebb of a wave on a beach. I had tried, and failed, and I was ashamed.

I heard a high-pitched yell in the courtyard. I rose to my knees and peered out the window. Four nuns were standing in the falling snow. I couldn't see their faces clearly because of the thick flakes, the poor illumination, my breath which kept misting the pane. One nun had thrown a snowball at another, who was laughing and pointing her finger accusatorially. She bent over and made her own snowball and threw it back at her assailant, who shrieked and dodged. And then they were all making snowballs and tossing them awkwardly at one another, laughing and running about like excited children. One tall nun scooped up a lapful of snow in her skirt. Making a chugging sound, she chased the one who'd started it all, who squealed and tried to escape, only to slip and fall in the snow. Her attacker flipped up her habit, dumping snow on her. Then they were all upon her, furiously shoveling snow with their hands. "No, no," she screamed, and laughed, and then they were all laughing, until one by one they collapsed, panting, their black habits powdered white with snow. For one moment, no one and nothing moved in the courtyard except the snow falling from far above and far away, and all of it—courtyard and snow and nuns—looked like a miniature scene in the snow globes I'd seen at the five-and-dime. *If I breathe*, I thought, *they will vanish.*

And then they rose, and brushed themselves off, and quietly walked across the courtyard and into the dark.

I heard voices in the hall, the loudest my father's. The door opened, and there he was. "Let's go," he said, his lips tight. We saw no one as we left.

We got into the car and drove away from St. Stanislaus. My father gripped the wheel tightly with both hands. The streets were silent except for the scrunch of our tires. "Goddam snow," he muttered. A muscle in his jaw twitched.

Everything looked different, I thought. The houses in the Third Ward seemed transformed, the cluttered yards now soft undulating hillocks of snow, the stripped cars fantastic caverns. A gutted deer hanging on a child's swing was magically rimed and glistening and frosted. Lights were on in the houses; people lived there after all.

"What happened?" my father asked. "What did those damn nuns say to you?"

"Nothing," I murmured, as I stared at the houses. Through one window I could see a man brushing his wife's hair with slow, gentle strokes; in another, a young couple danced languidly while a little boy drove a toy car around their legs. I thought: *I have never seen any of this before.* We crossed the bridge. It was too dark to see the river, but I knew it must be there also, and that below its ice, it was flowing, away from Tyler, and even though I didn't yet know its destination, still, my father was wrong—it was flowing somewhere.

"They must have said *something,*" my father said, looking at me hard. "They told me you were crying."

I didn't reply. The car seemed hot and close, and I rolled down my window a crack. The sliver of cold air felt bracing. I thought of the nuns playing in the snow. And I wondered: *Could Sister Benedict have been one of those nuns in the courtyard?* And I just hadn't seen, hadn't known? I thought and thought, but couldn't decide.

"Well, that's it," my father said, making a cutting motion with his hand. "No more piano lessons! You're through with that." He slapped the steering wheel. "I'll just have to have it out with your mother."

But I wasn't listening anymore at all. I laid my head against the window, and closed my eyes, and felt the rest of my life come rushing toward me, like the French River flowing back on itself, and I knew with a shiver approaching wonder that all of it would be both more terrible and more wondrous than anything I'd ever been told before.

Break-in

—Summer 1959

The *Ten Commandments* was playing again at the Katona Theater in Tyler, the Rifleman dispensed frontier justice on TV, Roberto Clemente was hitting home runs for the Pirates, and I was one of a gang of boys who broke into people's homes. We were fifteen years old—Tommy Kozella, Ira Dunn, his cousin Ricky Dunn, and me. Little Orphan Annie was fighting juvenile delinquents—"rat packs," she called them—in the comics, and that's who we imagined we were. We wore tight jeans rolled at the cuff and tucked our cigarets under the sleeves of our T-shirts; I spent a long time in front of the mirror, combing the crest of my ducktail to the exact arrogant height, while trying to avoid seeing the acne which flared angrily on my face. We couldn't drive, couldn't drink legally, and we had no girlfriends. Our life in crime seemed predestined.

Usually we broke in just by jimmying first-floor windows or pushing the screens back a bit—it was amazing how often people left their windows unlocked or open in those summers before air conditioning. Most of the doors probably would've been open too, but that wouldn't have been a proper break-in, just walking through a door. We rarely stole much. We rifled through drawers and cabinets and purses if they were lying around, sometimes finding cash, sometimes not. We'd take table radios, records, Conneaut Lake paperweights, Lake Erie fishing caps, almost anything that caught our fancy, no matter how stupid: once Tommy took a wall clock designed as a Coca-Cola cap, and another time we stole a mounted trophy of a huge sea-grouper. "He looks like Debbie Beasley," Ira said, gazing at the fish's thick lips. And then he puckered up and kissed them. We'd always take beer and liquor, and once Ira took a .30-06 rifle and some shells, which we urged him not to—it seemed *too* criminal somehow. We'd read about Charley Starkweather, who'd killed all those people—including his girlfriend's parents—in a crime spree across the Midwest, and even though we were housebreakers and criminals and had difficulties and trouble with *our* parents (or, in Ira's case, parent—his father was an alcoholic who abandoned his mother and him for months at a time, and was gone again that summer), we certainly didn't want to become like Charley Starkweather. At least not Ricky and Tommy and me. Ira, however, was obsessed with him, and had scrupulously followed the trial in the paper. But nothing ever came of Ira's rifle theft—we shot milk bottles with it a couple times down at the gravel pit, and that was all.

We regarded the things we stole as if they were souvenirs from dangerous forays into foreign countries and their exotic bazaars. And that's what those homes were for me—foreign countries which one entered at great peril and remained in at great risk, places of strange sights and smells to be explored by flashlight in the quiet voices reserved for the tombs and cathedrals I'd seen in my grade-school geography books. In searching their rooms, I'd try to imagine the lives of the mysterious people who lived there. I'd gaze at their photos, which gazed back at me from mantels and walls and china closets. I'd stare at their crucifixes and Saint Anthony medals, the badly colored prints of Jesus in the Garden of Gethsemane, the St. Stanislaus and Western Auto calendars hanging in kitchens and porches. I'd ponder the things they collected and held precious, arranged on tables and bookshelves and cupboards: glass angels, china animals, ceramic clowns, miniature teddy bears. One family had a collection of rabbits with golf clubs; another had a wall decorated with embroideries from the Wanango County Fairs of the last fifteen years. I'd look at their magazines—*Life, Good Housekeeping, Grit, Our Sunday Visitor*—and, more rarely, their books, most often Reader's Digest condensed books. I'd look through their refrigerators and drawers. I'd smell their closets, sometimes fragrant with sachet, often stuffy and stale. I'd finger their clothes. I'd look in their children's rooms and try to imagine who they were from their magazines and comic books, their toys, their models of ships or airplanes. Sometimes I felt I could see all of them more clearly than I could see my own parents—more clearly than I could see me.

We kept our booty on the upper level of Tommy's garage. His parents never came up there—his father had a bad hip and couldn't climb stairs very well, and his mother had a morbid fear of spiders and so never even went into the garage. We put the fish up on the wall and hid the gun and the liquor and other contraband in the rafters. We'd gather there summer evenings and play poker and smoke cigarets and drink our stolen liquor and beer (always warm, since we had no refrigerator to keep it in) while the sea-grouper glared down on us with his angry, gelatinous eye.

We searched for accounts of our crimes in the *News-Herald,* and were often disappointed. Almost always our break-ins weren't reported—sometimes I think that people hadn't even realized they'd been broken into, or, if they had, didn't bother to tell the police, since we usually never stole anything of great value. But occasionally our exploits were recorded, and we'd read the articles gleefully, and cut them out and keep them locked in the drawer of an old metal desk to which only Tommy had the key. The theft of the sea-grouper was one of those that made the *Herald*—evidently the fish was the prize trophy of one Earl Magruder from a fishing trip to Tarpon Springs, the only thing he'd *ever* caught in all his years of fishing. There was a reward and a plea from Magruder to return it. "He just loves that fish," his wife said in the article. Ira laughed and laughed, but I felt sorry for Magruder, and suggested that we return the fish, leave it by his door or something. Ira and Ricky said that was crazy, it had been dangerous enough getting the fish over to the garage that night, and they'd be damned if they'd risk carrying it back again, especially since its theft had been in the paper and everybody would be on the lookout for it now.

And then one day Ricky Dunn came whooping up the stairs, shaking a copy of the *Herald,* the paper flapping like pigeon wings. "Look at this!" he cried. "You guys've got to read this!"

We crowded around. There it was on page two, an article half a column long, headlined "Rash of Break-ins in Tyler." It described how Tyler police were certain that a string of burglaries in the past four months was the work of teenagers. " 'It's got all the hallmarks of kids,' " Chief Larry Coombs was quoted as saying. " 'They take alcohol, odds and ends. They don't seem interested in things a professional thief would take—silver, china, and the like.' "

"Silver. We got to steal some silver next time," Ricky said.

"What the fuck do we want with silver?" Ira asked.

"That's another thing. China. We should get some of that, too."

"Dishes," Ira snorted.

"Do they suspect anybody?" I asked.

Ricky put his finger on the column and read: " 'There are some leads,' Chief Coombs said. 'And there are some boys we've got our eyes on.' Other than that, Chief Coombs wouldn't speculate, other than to say that he expected the police would soon be making arrests."

"Jesus." Tommy whistled.

"I wonder if he thinks it's us?" Ricky said.

"How could he?" I said. "I mean, it's not like we've been in trouble before or anything."

"He's just bluffing," Ira said. "He probably don't have any leads at all. He's just saying that to spook whoever's doing it."

"That's us," Ricky said. "We're doing it."

"Well, it's spooked me," Tommy said. "Maybe we better stop."

"What if they *do* suspect us?" Ricky said. "I mean, maybe we left fingerprints or something."

"We oughta wear gloves," Ira said.

"Maybe there's some incriminating evidence," Tommy said. "Lieutenant Frank Ballinger said on 'M Squad' that a criminal always leaves some kind of evidence at the scene of the crime."

"Fuck Frank Ballinger," Ira said. "That's just TV."

"You don't know that, Ira," Tommy said. "They've got scientific instruments that can find things you never even knew about. Little hairs and things like that."

"They don't got that stuff here, Tommy," Ira said. "You think the cops here're like 'M Squad'? They probably don't even got a fingerprint kit, for Chrissake!"

Tommy held up his hands. "I'm out. I'm through with it."

"They probably got us under surveillance right now," Ricky said. He got up and began pacing. "We're gonna get sent to Mercersburg." That was the reform school some forty miles away, where we'd heard they shaved your head and made you work in the fields cultivating radishes and turnips.

Tommy cut out the clipping, unlocked the desk drawer, stuffed it in, and closed and relocked the drawer. "They're probably talking to our parents right now," he said.

"I've had it then," Ricky said. "My father'd say anything to send me away. They'd just have to give him the idea and he'd take it from there. 'Oh yeah, I saw that little pecker coming home the other night with a whole bag full of—what'd they steal? Silverware? Yeah, just *full* of silverware.'"

Everybody laughed nervously, and then we were silent. We contemplated Mercersburg.

And then I had my idea. "Okay," I said, "if they're suspicious about us, we'll throw them off the track."

"How, Frankie?" Ira asked. He was always calling me Frankie, as if I were some Chicago mobster. I didn't like it, but I never told him. Ira was tough to tell things to.

"We'll break into one of *our* houses."

"Why do we want to do that?" Ricky asked. "We already got what we got. What's to steal?"

"If we break into one of our houses, the cops'll never suspect us." And before I even realized I was going to say it: "We'll break into *my* house."

"Wack-o," Tommy said.

"No, it's good," Ira said. "I like it, Frankie." He lit a cigaret, dragged deeply and dramatically, just like Kookie on "77 Sunset Strip," and threw the match on the floor. "It's real good."

IT WAS AT LEAST a week before we could put my plan into action—it seemed my parents would never go out at the same time. But then on my father's league bowling night, my mother decided to play canasta at Elsa Mayhew's. I made a quick round of phone calls, and plans were set.

We met at the Pizza Parlor—Tommy too, reluctantly, under pain of forever being called a pansy-ass. After a pizza and a pitcher of Coke, we left in pairs, to reconnoiter in a half-hour behind my house. My parents had left a light on over the garage, but before I'd left, I'd turned it off, so no one could see us from the O'Connor house next door, which was dark anyway.

"Jesus, this is wack-o," Tommy said, as we pressed against the side of the garage. "I mean, it's *crazy.*"

"This is probably how Charley Starkweather did it," Ira said. "He crept up to houses and looked in the windows and then—" He shot Tommy with a mock pistol.

Ricky raised his eyebrows, as if to say, *This again.*

"I mean, it's *too* crazy," Tommy said. "I got a bad feeling about this, I gotta tell you."

"You got a bad feeling about everything," Ira said. "If you was Columbus, you'd never have gotten out of the dock. We'd all still be Indians." He pointed to me. "Not like Frankie." He grinned. "Frankie's got vision." I couldn't tell how he meant that. Ira was hard to read sometimes, and so a little scary. Ricky and Tommy, you usually knew what they were thinking. They'd tell you, or you could figure it out. Ira—no. We were friends, but I'm not sure we really liked each other.

"Let's just do it, okay?" Tommy said. Always before a break-in, there was this hesitation. You could either do it or not, and if you did, then you were a criminal again, and if you didn't, everything could be just as it always was, a lot safer, but no different.

"Everybody got their gloves on?" Ira asked. Just in case Chief Coombs *did* have a fingerprint kit, we'd decided to start wearing them. "Flashlights? Bags?" We dashed across the yard and sidled along the side of the house.

"How're we going to do this?" Ricky whispered.

"I left the kitchen window open," I said.

Ira shook his head. "No good. For this one, we got to do it right. We got to *really* break in. Smash a window."

"Why?" I asked. "We've never done that before."

"We got to throw off all suspicion it was an inside job. I mean, that's why we're doing it, right?"

He had a point.

While we watched, Ira took off his T-shirt and wrapped it tight around his hand. He knelt beside a basement window. "I seen a burglar do this on 'M-Squad,'" he told us. He waited for a car to pass on the street to mask the sound, and swung. The glass didn't break. He quickly swung again, harder, and this time the glass shattered. It made less noise than I thought it would, more a dull crackling, like flames spitting in a fire.

"This is real weird," Tommy said. "We never really *broke* in before."

Ira put his shirt back on. "You got to be prepared to go the extra mile." He reached through, unfastened the latch, pushed the window open. "Crime's like that."

"What the hell does that mean?"

But Ira was already on his back, shimmying through the open window.

"What does he mean, Frank?" Tommy asked me.

"Shut up," I said. "Let's go."

We wiggled through and dropped onto my father's workbench a few feet below. We went up the basement stairs and into the kitchen. The only light came from the illuminated Benrus clock over the stove. We were in my house, where we'd been so many times before, come not as visitors now, but as thieves.

"Keep the goddam flashlights off," Ira hissed.

"What now?" Tommy asked.

"I don't know," I said. "Steal stuff."

"*Silverware!*" Ricky said.

"Uh-uh. That's my mother's from my grandmother. We don't take that."

"China, then."

"We don't got china. Just A & P dishes."

Ricky opened the refrigerator and pulled out a Coke, just as he always did when he came to my house. "Hey—beer." He put the Coke back and pulled out a six-pack of Rolling Rock. He handed each of us one. I got a church key from the drawer, opened mine, and passed it around.

"Here's to crime," Ricky said. We toasted, and drank.

"Rolling Rock," Ira said. "The best."

"That what your father drinks?" Tommy asked.

Ira's face clouded for a moment, but then he laughed. "Sure. Why not?" He snapped his fingers. "Hey—your dad got any real booze, Frankie? We can take that."

I opened the cabinet where my father kept a bottle of Scotch and one of bourbon. He rarely drank either, preferring beer, but kept them on hand for guests. Every now and then I'd sneak nips out of the Scotch bottle, carefully refilling it with water. The bourbon had never been opened. I held them up triumphantly.

"All *riiight!*" Ricky said.

We went into the darkened living room and pulled down the shades. Ira's flashlight beam danced on the walls, the paisley sofa, the Dutch cupboard, the piano we'd moved in from the side porch, the reproduction of Millais's *Angelus* over the fireplace. Everything was the same but different somehow, as mysterious and frozen as stalagmites. "I don't think I've ever been in your house before, Frankie," Ira said. "It's real nice." It was true, I realized—for whatever reason, I'd never had Ira over here. But then again, I'd never been to his place, either—a small rented house behind a taxidermy shop in the Third Ward.

Ira opened the Scotch, took a swig, and followed it with a swig of beer. "Boilermaker," he told us. "This is what the steelworkers in Pittsburgh do."

We all followed suit. The Scotch hit me in a straight jolt somewhere behind my eyes and I thought I was breathing fire. Tommy coughed and coughed, and Ira and Ricky laughed.

Ricky turned on the TV.

"Hey," I said, "turn that off."

"I'll keep it low," Ricky said. "Besides, this gives us a little light, so we don't have to use the—hey, will you fucking look!"

There he was, ghostly in the TV darkness—Raj Kapoor at the organ. Raj was this very mysterious, very unsmiling Indian swathed in white robes and a white turban with a huge ruby in the center. He played with half-closed eyes, swaying slightly. He could've been charming snakes instead of playing the organ.

"I hate this guy," Ricky said. "My mother watches him all the time. She thinks he's dreamy."

"A real greaseball," Ira said.

"What I'm going to ask you is this," Ricky said. "Why does everything he play sound like accordion music? I mean, he's playing a goddam organ, for Chrissake."

"It's not like it sounds like an *accordion,*" Tommy said. "It's just that all his songs sound like 'Lady of Spain.'"

"Hey, you're right! That's it exactly."

"I dig Ed Sullivan anyway," Tommy said.

"And now we've got a *reeeally . . . big . . . sheeww* for you," Ricky mimicked. He hunched his shoulders, interlocked his fingers, and cracked them. He did great imitations—his Elmer Fudd and Elliot Ness were the best.

"Too many goddam circus acts," Ira said. He took another pull of Scotch. "Dogs and jugglers. Boring."

"They had a magician on last week who was pretty good," Tommy said. "He put a girl in a box and when he opened it up, a flock of pigeons came out."

"That trick's so old," I said.

"Matter of fact, the guy looked like Raj Kapoor."

"I need that box for my old man," Ira said. He crumpled his beer can and carefully put it on the coffee table.

"He disappears okay without it, seems to me," Tommy said. I caught Tommy's eye in the strange half-light from the TV, and shook my head slightly. But Ira hadn't heard him, or at least didn't say anything.

"Wouldn't it be great," I said, "to have a box where you could go in and open it up and be somewhere else?"

"Just where would you like to go?" Ira asked.

I shrugged.

"Disappearing's no good if you don't know where you're going," Ira said.

We contemplated that.

Ira lifted the bottle of Scotch, and shone his flashlight

through it. He twirled the bottle. Liquid amber light danced on the walls.

"That's pretty," Ricky said.

Ira put down the flashlight and took another swig. "We gotta get cooking," he said, and passed the Scotch to Tommy.

"But *fiiirst,* before they commit the *criiime,"* Ricky said, still imitating Ed Sullivan, "they're going to have another *rouuund.*"

"We better not get plowed," I said.

We passed the bottle around. Raj was playing "April in Paris." "Turn that damn swami off," Ricky said, but no one moved. Things were already starting to blur around the edges. Ricky took a deep swig and leaned back against the sofa. "You know, my mother told me something really wild the other day. She—"

"She told you you were Crazy Harry's son," Ira said. Tommy and I laughed. Crazy Harry was a short, fat man who wandered around Tyler smiling and mumbling to himself. He always walked in a very determined way, arms swinging precisely, just like Alec Guinness in *The Bridge on the River Kwai.*

"She told me," Ricky said, "that some old geezer came into the emergency room"—Ricky's mother was a nurse at Memorial Hospital—"gasping and wheezing away, having a heart attack or something. So they get him up on the table, and they rip off his clothes to goose him and everything, and you know what they find?"

"He's wearing women's underwear," Tommy said.

Ricky looked amazed, then crestfallen. "How'd you know that?"

"Really? That's it? I just said that."

"Well, you're right. He was wearing a girdle and everything."

"Jesus." Ira whistled. "A flit."

"Maybe that's why he was having the heart attack," I said. "His girdle was too tight." We all laughed.

"I don't know if he was a flit," Ricky said. "I mean, he was an old man and everything."

"Age don't make no difference," Ira said. "You heard about dirty old men, right?"

"My mom says he was probably just wearing it like a truss or something. You know, something to hold a hernia in. She says you'd be surprised how many men wear women's underwear."

"I've never understood women's underwear," Tommy said. "I mean, how can they *wear* that stuff?"

"Girls don't," I said. "It's just old women that wear girdles."

"My mother ain't old," Tommy said, "and she wears one. How about your mother, Frank?"

"I don't know," I said, flushing.

"She wears one, I bet," Ira said. "Women with class wear them."

"Sure," I said. "I suppose." I was a little embarrassed, but pleased he thought my mother had class. Ira didn't give too many compliments. He took another swig of the Scotch. When he tried to put the bottle on the coffee table, he missed, scraping the edge. He squinted, as if taking a bead on bottle and table, and put it down once more, carefully.

"And *nowww*, here's *Iraah Dunn*," Ricky announced, "and he's a *lit-ttle, teensy* bit drunk—"

"It's funny," Ira said. "Some women, you just look at them, you know they got class. I don't know what it is. Something about the—*hair* or something. I mean, it's just something you can *see*."

"It's the fingernails," Ricky said. "If they're clean or not. That's the giveaway."

"I never thought of that," Ira murmured. He shone the flashlight on his hand to examine the nails.

"Now Linda McIlhenny, she's got class," Tommy said.

"Debbie Beasley," Ricky said. "There's a whore."

"How would you know?" Ira asked. His voice was slurred, yet edgy. "You don't know shit about Debbie Beasley. Debbie Beasley, she—" He stopped and was silent.

"Hey," Ricky said. "I thought you didn't like her."

Ira picked up the Scotch bottle, pressed it to his cheek, closed one eye, and peered at us through it. "You all look funny," he said. And then the bottle slipped from his grasp, and there it was, Scotch all over the carpet.

"I knew that was gonna happen," I said. "I just *knew* it."

"Sorry," Ira mumbled.

"Good thing we got another bottle," Ricky said, holding up the bourbon.

"Boy, I'm going to get it," I moaned. "Jesus."

"Hey, Frank." Ricky snapped his fingers. "Are you thinking or what? It's not us, remember? It's the *burglars.*"

He was right: it wasn't us at all. I would get away with this. The world seemed to spin and swirl—not just from liquor, but with the awful possibilities of crime and its freedom.

"Charley Starkweather," I said. "That's us."

"You guys"—Ira wagged his finger—"ain't worthy to lick Charley Starkweather's ass."

"Will you fuck Charley Starkweather?" Tommy said. "I'm sick of hearing about that nut case. Jesus, he killed his parents, for God's sake!"

"He didn't kill his parents," Ira said. "He killed his *girl-friend's* parents."

"So big difference."

"If Charley Starkweather was here," Ira said, "he'd blow you all away." He pointed his finger like a pistol at Tommy.

"Bam—gone." He turned it on Ricky. "Bam—gone. A bunch of flits." He held his finger longer on me, then pulled the trigger. "Bam," he said softly.

"You are goddam *spooky*, Ira," Tommy said. "You ought to be committed."

"Mercersburg, for sure," Ricky said.

"I'd like to blow away my old man," Ira said. Again he aimed, as if his father were sitting in the armchair across the room. "Blam! Get both of them, one blast, the old man *and* the old lady."

"It's great to see that kind of love," Tommy said. "It's heart-warming."

Ricky cracked open the bourbon and we passed it around. The evening was getting murkier, as if a gauze were coming between me and everything else, a gauze I could not only see, but feel. It covered my hands and fingertips so that nothing felt quite real. I rolled my tongue around my mouth, trying to lick off the gauze which seemed to coat it, too.

"What're you thinking, Frank?" Ricky asked. "You're real quiet."

"I don't know," I said. And then: "I can't get over feeling we should clean up the booze."

"You don't got the true criminal mind, Frankie," Ira said. "You think you're bad, but you're not." He looked at me appraisingly. "You could do anything, you know. *Be* anything. You got vision."

I shrugged uncomfortably.

"What's your old man want you to do?" Ira asked.

"I don't know," I said. "I don't think he thinks I can do much of anything."

It was true—I didn't know what my father wanted of me, nor expected, if indeed he expected anything. With each passing year, I seemed to know him less. He seemed to become ever more silent, his attention focused inward, as if he'd forgotten something important and was trying hard to remember. He came home from the bearing plant, turned on "Douglas Edwards with the News," read the *Herald,* and after dinner settled down with more TV. That's how I thought of him mostly, sitting heavily in the beige armchair, chin resting on his chest, as if he were ready to nod off. Weekends, he'd putter around the house, fixing a lamp, sharpening the lawn-mower blades, caulking the tub and sink. He liked to fix things and was disappointed and somewhat exasperated that I didn't. He took pride in keeping his workbench neat, the tools carefully hung up or stored away. He'd berate me for the slovenliness of my room, and we'd argue, and often my mother would have to intervene to make peace.

"My old man wants me to be a vet," Ricky said. "He thinks I got a way with animals. It's cause I had an ant farm once."

"What about you, Tommy?" Ira asked.

"Be a barber at Pop's shop, I guess." He grinned. "I mean, that's what I'm supposed to be, right?"

"What do you mean?" Ira spread his arms. "This is *America.* You can be anything you want."

"Well, what's wrong with being a barber, Ira?"

"All I mean is, you don't *got* to be one."

"I don't know." Tommy shrugged. "Hair's okay."

"What about you, Ira?" I asked.

He looked at me. "I'm gonna be Charley Starkweather the Second. And then I'm gonna be dead."

For some reason, maybe because we were three-quarters drunk, we all thought this terribly funny. We laughed and laughed. On the TV, Raj was winding up at the organ. He stood up and solemnly took a bow.

"That's it, asshole," Ricky said to the TV screen. "Now get on your elephant and ride."

"Back to the Taj-fucking-Mahal," Tommy said.

"Jesus." Ira sighed deeply and hiccupped. "We're just sitting around, getting plastered. We gotta get going. We got *crime* to commit."

"Maybe we should just forget about this." I said it before I even knew I was thinking it.

"Frankie," Ira said, "this was *your* idea. You're not chickening out, are you?" He was smiling, but there was that wild, hard look in his eye that made me uneasy. When Ira looked at you that way, he was hard to deny.

"No," I said.

"Well, come on then." He took another swig of bourbon and wiped his lips. He rose unsteadily. I was feeling lightheaded, syrupy. When I got up, the room swirled a little, as if I'd just ridden the Tilt-a-Whirl at Conneaut Lake, and I had to lean on the sofa for a moment for support. As if on signal, we all turned on our flashlights. The beams danced giddily around the walls, the ceiling. Ricky giggled.

"Let's *do* something already," Tommy said.

"We gotta think like this is some stranger's place," Ira said. "We gotta get out of the head that this is your house, Frankie."

Tommy and I stayed downstairs while Ricky and Ira went up. I looked around. Somehow, as we'd been sitting there drinking, my house stopped seeming as strange and magical as the others we'd broken into. Was there anything really worth stealing here, after all?

"How about those?" Tommy pointed to a pair of porcelain Chinese doves in the Dutch cupboard. And I thought, no, I couldn't do that, my mother really liked them.

"Forget it," I told him.

"What then? You tell me."

For the life of me, I didn't know what to steal. It was hard to look at your own house the way a thief would. We took a toaster and blender from the kitchen. There was no sentimentality, no feeling associated with kitchen appliances, and they could be easily replaced.

We stumbled drunkenly up the stairs and went into my room. Our flashlights poked along the bureau, the chest of drawers, the card table where I did my homework. I tried to look at my room the way I looked at those of other houses we broke into. I tried to piece together who this kid was, what he was interested in, was he anybody I'd want to know. There was an old record player on the desk and a pile of 45's. I sorted through them: Paul Anka, Elvis Presley, Richie Valens. *Likes rock 'n' roll,* I thought. I looked at the books: a dictionary, an atlas, star maps, myths and legends of ancient Greece. I looked at the photos on the wall of Halley's comet, Saturn, the moon, big postcards really, bought on an eighth-grade class trip to the planetarium in Pittsburgh. *Likes staring into space,* I thought. My flashlight passed over the travel posters on the opposite wall, Capri and Switzerland and Greece. I opened bureau drawers and looked at the cufflinks I'd been given as a gift by Aunt Grace and never worn, liras and francs and drachmas from a coin collection at age nine. Underneath the lining of the drawer was an old, never-used condom, hard as a gumball, I got from Terry Tidwell. Ira would tease me unmercifully if he knew.

I thought: *If this was the room of a stranger, would I want to take anything at all?*

"Maybe the record player?" Tommy suggested, as if reading my thoughts.

I shook my head. "It's got a blown tube or something.

You crank up the volume all the way, it hardly makes a sound."

"A thief wouldn't know that," Tommy said. "He'd just take it."

He had a point.

"Besides"— he grinned mischievously—"this is the way to get a new one."

As we unplugged it and closed the cover, I felt as if I were going to be sick. "I'm going downstairs," I said. "I just remembered something." If I was going to vomit, I didn't want to do it in the upstairs bathroom, where they all could hear. I stumbled downstairs and sat heavily on the bottom step. I breathed deeply. Just being alone for a moment made me feel better, and the nausea passed.

I saw the Dutch cupboard where my father kept his papers. I rose and rummaged through the drawers. They were full of letters, insurance papers, old checkbooks, clippings from the *News-Herald*'s "Handyman" column. One drawer was locked, and I'd always wondered what was in it. Well, I was a thief now—I could find out. I jimmied it with my jackknife, tugged, jimmied again, and yanked. The drawer snapped open. It was stuffed with photos. I riffled through pictures of my parents and me at company barbecues, the Fireman's Fair, Conneaut Lake. Further down were older photos—some from before my mother and father had married. In one, my mother was at a swimming pool, too small for the number of young men and women frolicking in it. She wore a bathing cap and smiled shyly. She seemed to be the only one aware that the camera was there. My father wasn't in that picture at all. In another, they were linked arm-in-arm, the sun striking them from an odd angle so that their faces were harsh ridges and planes of sunlight and shadow. The day must have been cold—my mother had the fur collar of her jacket turned up, and my father's service uniform was buttoned to his throat. He was wearing gloves, she wasn't. Her hands, even from so far away in space and time, seemed chapped.

I had never seen these photos before. Why did my father feel he had to lock them away? And from whom, I wondered, if not from me?

Another photo—and this one I stared at for a long time. My father was standing in the parking lot of a place that looked like a Howard Johnson's on a turnpike. Cars were going by in the background, and it was summer. He seemed younger than in the photo with my mother, and he was holding a golf club, which was strange, since he didn't play golf at all, and as far as I knew, never had. And what could he be doing with a golf club on a highway anyway? But the most amazing thing was that he was laughing, something he rarely seemed to do anymore, head tossed to one side, hair falling boyishly across his forehead. A breeze rippled his shirt.

This is before everything, I thought. Before he married my mother—probably before he even met her—and it was not here, not Tyler, but somewhere else. The space behind him spoke of distances, not the enclosing hills of western Pennsylvania, and the cars spoke of movement across a vastness which he confronted with a toss of his head, a golf club, and a laugh.

I put the picture in my pocket.

I heard shrieks of laughter from my parents' room, Ricky's the loudest. I went upstairs. Ricky was rolling on the bed, howling. "L-l-look!" he whooped.

Ira had put on one of my mother's bras and girdles and was mincing around the room. Ricky and Tommy trained their flashlights on him. He put his hand behind his head and pursed his lips in a lascivious *moue.*

"Hel-looo, baa-by!" Ricky said, like the Big Bopper singing "Chantilly Lace."

"Do you boys love me?" Ira asked in a trilling falsetto. He batted his eyelashes coquettishly. "Do you *really* love me?"

Ricky shrieked.

"Jesus," I said. "Keep it down."

"*Well do you wanna dance?*" Tommy sang, holding his flashlight like a microphone, the upwardly angled light making his face almost ghoulish—"*under the mooonnnlight—*"

"*—kiss me baby,*" Ira picked it up, "*all through the night—*"

"Oh, we have a *reeeally* big *sheeww* for you tonight," Ricky said. "A *reeally* big *sheeww.*"

"C'mon, you guys," I said. "Ira, take off that goddam stuff." Seeing him in my mother's clothes bothered me.

"I *want* them!" he protested. "I *like* them."

"Come on, Ira. They're my mom's."

Ira took off the bra. "I'm gonna take this," he said thickly. His eyes shone hard. The headlights of a car on the street made shadows pass crazily along the ceiling and down the walls.

"Okay, take it." I threw up my hands. "Be a flit, who cares?"

"I'm gonna take this"—he twirled the bra around his finger—"and practice with it, so's when I get Debbie Beasley—"

"Look," I said. "Let's get out of here."

"What've we got?" Ricky asked drunkenly.

"We got a radio," Tommy said, "a toaster—"

"—a bra, a girdle—"

"Let's bug *outta* here," I said.

When we trooped down the stairs, Ricky missed a step and tumbled down. He lay sprawled at the bottom.

"Make enough noise there, Ricky?" Tommy asked.

"Jesus," he groaned. "I'm *hurt.*"

"The booze," Ira said.

Ricky waved the bottle triumphantly.

"My God, you didn't break it," Tommy said. "A fucking miracle."

We went back to the living room. The TV was still on. "Let's have another round before we go," Ira said. We passed the bourbon around, and took quick hot swigs. The fumes made my nose tingle and burn, and I coughed, and coughed again. The room seemed ever more off-center, unhinged.

Tommy raised the bottle. "To crime."

"To Charley Starkweather!" Ricky said.

Another car passed by, so loudly that for a moment it sounded as if it were going to pull into the drive. My heart skipped. The lights raked across the living room and were gone.

And then the strangest thing happened. We all seemed to turn at once and, in the blue-green half-light cast by the TV, saw ourselves in the mirror over the mantel. Maybe it was the booze, or the night, or crime itself, but it was like turning a corner in the fun house at Conneaut Lake and seeing yourself in one of those distorting mirrors, and you're startled, because for a moment you don't know who it is, and then you laugh, and shake your head and say, "Jesus, that's me!" It was us, and we all looked distorted. I saw Tommy, confused and blinking; and Ricky smiling like Crazy Harry; and Ira, tense and alert. And me—I had a dumb, wondering look on my face, and I thought, *That's how you really look, just like a dumb, pimply kid.* And I saw the craziness of it all: there was nothing, nothing worth stealing. We had a toaster we'd never use, a bra, some booze which we'd probably soon throw up, a busted record player. A photo. It was like taking dust from the air, air from a vacuum, silence from an empty room. It was the simplest problem in freshman algebra: nothing from nothing was still nothing.

We'd been dreaming, I thought. Crime was nothing more than dreaming that things could be different. Ricky and Tommy could stop breaking in next week and it would be all right, because they never really understood or felt that dream. Ira, however, did dream—of something unreclaimable, violent, that he would rage against until it brought him down and he, too, stopped dreaming.

And me—what did I dream? In that moment of drunken, swirling clarity, I thought I knew.

I dreamed I would be gone. I would leave Tyler. I would leave them all.

Ira caught my eye in the mirror, and for a moment, I felt he understood all of this too, our fate and our futility. In the end, he was the one I knew best, and I'd just never seen it before, nor wanted to. We were criminals, we were dreamers. We were brothers. And we hated one another.

"I hate that TV," Ira said calmly. He threw the empty Scotch bottle. The screen shattered with a hiss. Everything— time, space, the evening—seemed to crystallize around the sound of that glass breaking. We stared stupefied at the glowing, dying tube in the center of the set. Tommy whistled softly. In the semidarkness, Ira was looking at me. *Could you have done this?* his eyes seemed to say. *Could you even have dared?*

I picked up the bourbon bottle and threw it against the wall. It shattered, splattering the remaining liquor. And then we were all knocking over furniture and breaking things. Tommy picked up a dining-room chair and smashed it against the floor, again and again, until it broke, then smashed another. Ricky picked up a vase and dropped it, and it shattered too. Ira was in the kitchen now, pulling down the spice rack, opening jars and spilling the contents on the floor. We whooped and we cried and we abandoned ourselves to pillage and cared no more for stealth and its secrecies, and I knew with one part of my mind that what we were doing was crazy, crazy, and I think I even said so, but we did it anyway. The abandonment to destruction was as sweet as any abandonment to love.

"Just *look* at what they're *doing!*" Ricky was saying in his Ed Sullivan voice. He had a broom and was poking holes in the plasterboard of the kitchen ceiling. "It's a—*reeeallly* big *sheeww.*"

And then we were stumbling out the back door into the darkness. We ran in panic and excitement, snorting for air. We would be caught, I knew we would be caught, already I imagined sirens in the night. And then we were at the Pizza Parlor parking lot, and we stopped running and leaned against the wall, gasping for breath.

"Jesus," Ricky said, and Tommy said, "Fucking A."

"My God, am I shit-faced," Ricky said. And then yelled, "I'm *shiiit-faaaced!*"

"Shut up," I said. "Goddammit."

"They're gonna catch us," Tommy moaned. He slid down the wall to the ground. "They're gonna get us for sure."

"What about the stuff?" Ira asked. "Who's got the stuff?"

We stared at each other. In our excitement and panic, we'd left the booty behind. I felt in my pocket—the photo of my father was still there.

"Jesus," Ira groaned. "A bunch of flits."

And I thought, *Any moment we will hear sirens.* Red lights would be flashing, and we'd throw up our hands in surrender. *Okay,* I'd say. *You got me.* We'd be brought down to the police station, where I'd only been twice before—once when I was nine to get a license for my bike and last year when my father paid a traffic ticket. But now I'd be there as a burglar and a vandal. They'd book me and fingerprint me and shove me around like in "M Squad," and then we'd be put in jail. My mother and father would be summoned, and I'd be brought out, a police radio squawking in the background. My father would look at me, head shaking grimly, and my mother would be crying, hand to her mouth, her eyes pleading, *Why?*

Could I say why? Could I demand that my father tell me why he was no longer the man in the photograph? Could I take my mother's hand and tell her I was afraid and ashamed of the very defiance I felt? Could I tell them that in the shattering of a window, the breaking of a TV screen, the whole world could change? You could be free. You could die out there. You could be gone.

Governotou

—*Summer 1969*

The summer after I turned twenty-five I lived in Réthimnon, on the north coast of Crete, in a room above the offices of *O Ilios,* the Communist newspaper. I'd come there for reasons that were at once both clear and eccentric. I'd never been to Europe, and from childhood Greece had represented everything mystical and strange. I'd been fascinated by its myths; I'd stared at the engraved portraits of Plato and Aristotle and Demosthenes on the drachmas in my coin collection; for years I'd had a poster of Delphi on my wall at home, and later on my wall in college. "You have the soul of an Athenian," a philosophy professor once wrote on a paper, and while I knew he was joking, I thought it might also be a sign. Greece was where mysteries of the spirit and flesh could happen, and I was ready for them to happen to me.

35

Since college, I'd been drifting. I'd taught English for a year in a Philadelphia inner-city school, then worked as a proposal writer for a community action project there. None of my proposals were funded, however, and after eight months, I was let go. I got a job as a writer for an agency that formulated standardized achievement tests for students, and I'd been there ever since. I wrote the English questions, grade levels six through eight. It was a horrible job, but it required little and did allow me a draft deferment. And then my position was "relined"— that's how they phrased it to me. I understood, without their actually saying so, that they wouldn't inform my draft board of my changed status till the fall. Until then, I was free.

And so was born the idea of Greece. I had some money saved. I would go live on an island, like Nicholas Urfe in *The Magus,* a favorite book. I would grow a beard, have love affairs in the Mediterranean sun. And I would write a novel. Even though I'd only written a few poems in college, and nothing since then, I felt in my soul I might be a writer. All I needed was time and a place far away from my life as it was. Greece would provide this: it would teach and transform me. My past would be past, and I would be reborn to a destiny—I actually thought the word—as clear as the glassy waters of the Aegean.

Before I left, I visited Tyler. I'd lost track of many of my old friends. Some had moved away, or were entwined in young marriages and young children—Ricky Dunn, for instance. ("It's not so great," he told me of his infant son, "but he's worth a deferment.") Ricky's cousin Ira had disappeared, just the way his father always had—there were rumors he'd gone to Alaska, or had joined the Marines and was in Vietnam. I was the only one who'd gone to college, and now, when I told Tommy Kozella at the barber shop—he'd indeed become a barber like his father— that I was going to Greece to write, he smiled and shook his head and said he wished he could go, too. And I smiled, but with the relief of someone who's escaped a great calamity.

Not everyone was enthusiastic about my going.

"It's the craziest thing I ever heard of," my father said. "Crete! Just what the hell are you going to do there?"

"Write," I said.

"Write? Write what?"

"A book. A novel."

He snorted. "You ought to just forget that idea. You got no business there."

"Why? Don't you think I can?"

"That's not what he means, Frank," my mother said.

"That's what he *said*, Mom!"

"I don't understand," my father said, "why you don't just marry Jena and settle down." Jena was the woman in Philadelphia I'd been seeing for the past year, whom my father liked very much. "Just forget all this craziness."

"It's not crazy!"

My mother looked fretful, as she always did when my father and I argued, but said nothing more. In some unacknowledged way, I felt, she approved of my going. Earlier she'd asked me questions about Crete's climate, geography, history. "That's where that monster was, right?"

"The Minotaur," I said.

"Yes. That one." Her eyes shone a bit, as if he might still be there.

And then there was Jena. On the drive to the airport we'd argued terribly. Parked in the rain in front of the Olympia Airways entrance, the car's wipers methodically slapping and squeaking, we'd argued more.

"It's only for the summer," I told her. "This'll be *good*. It'll give us time to think."

"You don't want to think at all." Her eyes were filmy, but she wouldn't cry, she was too proud for that. "You want to forget me."

"Jena, that's not true," I said, although in a way, if I'd been honest with myself, it was. I loved her, I thought, but lately she'd been pressing for us to live together, and I knew without her telling me that what she really wanted was to get married. In no way did I feel ready for that.

"I had a friend," she said, gripping the top of the steering wheel. "She waited four years for her boyfriend to make up his mind. And then he did. He married somebody else. That's what thinking does." She looked at me hard. "I'm not going to be that way. You better believe me."

I held her hand. A cop on the curb yawned and looked at his watch. "He wants us to move," I said, although he looked like he could care less. A skycap knocked on the window and pointed to my bags in the back seat, but before I'd even shaken my head, Jena shouted, "We don't need it, go away!" I scolded her for being rude, and we fought about *that* for a while. And then I said it really was time, I had to go, I'd write her, I'd be back soon, I'd think about us.

"Don't say 'think,'" she said. "If you say that one more time, I'll scream."

And then in an awful and awkward attempt to placate her and free myself and salve my conscience, I said, "Maybe we'll get married when I get back."

"No, we won't." She gave a small, sharp laugh. "I wouldn't *want* to marry you! Someone as selfish as—"

"Jesus, Jena!" I cried. "Can't you just make this *nice*!"

"Go on." She wouldn't look at me. "Go think."

I grasped her hand again. "I love you," I said. I leaned over and kissed her. Her cheek felt hot. I got out, and when I waved from the curb, she was already driving away.

Ten minutes later, as the gate attendant at Olympic Airways was looking at my passport, I thought, *Maybe we will get married.* I thought that again on the plane, somewhere over the Atlantic. And then I didn't think about it anymore at all.

I'D BEEN ON CRETE six weeks and all I had written, besides a few pages of a novel entitled *Labyrinth* about a young man who goes to Greece (and what else? I had no idea), were a few postcards to my parents and some letters to Jena. The walls of my room above the paper were gray from paper dust and printer's ink that seeped up from the presses below. By day I'd hear the chatter and shouting and cursing of the staff, who always seemed to be in crisis about something; at night the presses ran in a slow subterranean slur that made me feel I was sleeping in the bowels of an aged tramp steamer. I had no kitchen, just a hot plate which I never used, since its plug was cracked and I was afraid of electrocution. And the weather was stifling—the hottest summer on record, everyone said. For all these reasons, I hardly spent any time in my room. Mornings, I'd go to a *kafenion* and drink American coffee—the cups were bigger than the Greek kind—eat yogurt and honey, and read the *International Herald Tribune.* Mostly I felt like going back to sleep, the coffee and the sea breeze having a soporific, rather than invigorating, effect. Afternoons I went to the beach, or strolled through the Old Town. In the evening I went to the Bar Odostopolous along with other young people, students mostly, who were passing through Réthimnon with their backpacks, bandanas, Gitanes, and *Guide Bleus.* A sign outside promised "psykodelik musick" and "freakfast"—breakfast. Given the clientele, I thought that was very funny. I rarely saw anybody in the Odos before dinnertime, however, and it didn't really come alive until eleven or so, after people had eaten at the tavernas and then come over to the bar for the pinball, a little bored dancing, and the hope of picking somebody up. And it was there I heard about the abandoned monastery at Governotou.

I was sitting with two Swedes, Magnus and Karl, whom I'd just met, and Bitters, a German whom I didn't really like but with whom I wound up drinking many nights, since he too was in Réthimnon for the summer, attached to an archeological project restoring the Fortezza that overlooked the harbor. Bitters was in a state of continual sexual frustration. "The Greek girls you can't meet, the Germans and French all have disease, the English want you to pay for everything." He'd wave his hand and shrug. "You can have this place."

He was a bore, but then I probably bored him too.

My mind had been wandering—I was on my third or fourth beer, I'd slept badly the night before in the sweltering heat—when I heard Magnus say, ". . . and then the most amazing thing." He tamped his unlit cigaret dramatically on the edge of the table. "I was resting in this little chapel, just napping, when I hear this sound." He cocked his head, raised his eyebrows. "Someone is coming! Such a surprise—it has been so quiet, you know, no one else there at all. And then these two girls—Danish, you know—come through the doorway."

"Where was this?" I asked.

Magnus looked at me. His eyes were hooded, his lips full. There was something slow and heavy about him, which right now might seem sensual and attractive to women, but in a few years would turn thick and stolid. I didn't really like him, either, but there we all were, English speakers gathered together by language for the evening.

"The monastery at Governotou," he said.

"Frankie," Bitters said with a sigh, "haven't you been listening?"

"No. What monastery? Where's Governotou?"

"About forty kilometers from here," Magnus said. "There's the village, and then you must walk down a gorge to the monastery."

"Abandoned," Bitters added.

"An abandoned monastery?"

"Since the seventeenth century," Magnus said. "It is the strangest thing."

"Forget all this," Bitters said. "Tell about the girls."

"What's it like?" I asked. The image of an abandoned monastery in a deep gorge, already magnified in my mind to a wild chasm, enchanted me.

"You must walk for some half-hour along the side of this gorge," Magnus said, "and then suddenly you come around a turn, and it is there below you. Steps cut into the cliff lead down to it. On either side are ruins of the old buildings. The façade is preserved very well. A stone bridge crosses the river, which runs out to the sea. Below the bridge is a cave. They say that the bones of a hermit—Saint John the Stranger, I think his name is—are buried there."

"The *girls*," Bitters urged. He waved to the waiter for another round of Spartans.

Magnus smiled. "I was in this little traveler's chapel cut into the side of the cliff. There was a blue wooden table. On it, a soda bottle with dried flowers and a bowl of coins that visitors had left as offerings. A few cheap icons on the wall. A few chairs. That was all. I was just resting there when they came in. Students, about eighteen and nineteen, I should think. One with red hair, short, very big-bosomed. She did all of the talking, very lively, flirty, you know. The other was taller, long blond hair, almost white, and very shy, said not a word, just every now and then laughed a little, as if she had just thought of something funny, but only to herself, you know? The red-haired one said they'd been trying to find the tomb of Saint John the Stranger, but had no luck. She said they had to make the ferry to Piraeus that evening, that this was their last night on Crete. They'd been everywhere, she said. The monastery at Governotou was the last thing they would see.

"We smoked some grass, and then the red-haired one—I don't remember either of their names—said that she was going to look around a bit more, and I thought the other would go too, the blonde, but she stayed." Magnus interlocked his fingers and stretched his arms. "I was thinking, how terrible, I'm left alone with this one who is mute, while the other, you know, the one I'm interested in, has gone, and I think, maybe I'll just get up and follow her. So I say to the blonde maybe I'll help her friend find the cave, and she nods, and I go outside, but I can't see her friend at all. I call out, but no answer, and I'm a little bit worried, you know, because the footing is tricky there, one could fall. I go back into the chapel, thinking I'll get the blonde and we'll both go look—and what do you think?" He looked at Bitters and me, not at Karl, who had a small smile and was running his finger around the mouth of his beer—he'd heard this story before.

"She is lying there on the table, all her clothes off." Magnus smiled. "Completely naked."

"You liar," Bitters muttered. Magnus shook his head, almost sadly, as if he had encountered this disbelief before.

"Believe me, I am amazed too. We have hardly spoken, you know. If anything, I am thinking . . ." He paused, his eyes seeming to lose their focus for a moment in the Odos's smoky air.

"And?" Bitters said. "What happened?"

Magnus sighed. "What do you think? We fucked."

"I don't believe any of this," Bitters snorted.

"She never said a word," Magnus said, ignoring him. "At

one point she swept her arm and knocked over the vase, and the flowers spilled out on the table, and I could smell them, as if they were alive."

It was true, I thought. All of it, true.

Governotou, I said to myself.

Magnus closed his eyes. And I saw something in him I hadn't seen before, an urge, a yearning to touch and retouch this memory, as if he himself weren't quite sure it had happened, and only through its retelling could it become real again—the girl, the chapel, the odor of sage mixed with fine sweat, the hurried moans and sighs, her arm making a slow arc and knocking over the dead flowers, the nervousness that the friend would reappear through the still open door beyond which all the sun of Crete beat down on the gorge and the river below. I could see it all.

This is why I have come here, I thought.

"So what happened then?" Bitters asked. "As if I believe any of this."

Magnus lit another cigaret. "We got dressed. We heard her friend whistling outside, tramping back up the path. She made a lot of noise. I think she knew what we'd been doing." He shrugged. "Maybe they'd planned it even, some kind of code between them. Who knows? We all smoked a little more grass, and then went down to the river to swim. I fell asleep, and when I woke, they were gone."

He shifted his heavy body and folded his hands, considering them as if they were not hands at all but something else—his story, his life.

"Ah," Bitters groaned. "Why don't these things happen to me?"

"You have to be there," Magnus said. "You must be ready." He looked at me. "You should write about that," he said. "It's a good story, isn't it?"

"Frank doesn't write pornography." Bitters clapped me on the shoulder. "Frank writes only serious literature."

"You don't know what I write," I snapped. And to Magnus: "How do you get to this monastery? I'd like to see it."

"There's a path from the village," Magnus said. "Just ask there. Everyone knows it."

Later Bitters and I walked through the narrow streets of the Old Town. Cats foraged for scraps among the tables of the shuttered tavernas. The only sounds were the humming of the electric wires and a faraway motor scooter that snarled like a maddened hornet.

"Such a bullshitter," Bitters said. He laughed. "You don't believe any of that story, do you?"

"I don't know," I said.

"If you do, you're as big a fool as he is." He let out a great shout, something in German I didn't understand, and threw his beer bottle high in the air. It caught the streetlight and fell and shattered dully on the pavement behind us, and I thought how much I disliked Bitters, how glad I would be to see him go.

Governotou, I said under my breath. And shivered slightly, as if something cool and wondrous had blown through my soul.

I'VE HEARD A fantastic story about an abandoned monastery in the mountains, I wrote Jena. *There's the body of a hermit saint buried in a cave underneath the chapel, and at night the ghosts of the monks walk down the gorge bearing candles.* I fabricated this, of course—after all, I was a writer. What really happened to Magnus, I didn't say. I looked up from my letter and stared at the clouds piled over the harbor. They seemed high and mysterious, the sun slanting and glistening through them like canyons, not air and water at all, but possessed of a substantiality

I'd never before imagined, as if the very thought of Governotou could make one see everything anew.

But before I could even send this letter, I received one from Jena. *I don't want to hear anymore about the damn ocean and the goddam Venetian harbor and the ouzo and all that other crap,* she wrote. *It's all just geography. I can't find us anywhere in this. I can't even find* you *there. If you can't write something that means anything, then don't write at all. I'm tired of missing you. I'm tired of thinking about us for both of us.*

And then the final line: *You might as well know I've started seeing somebody else.*

I tore her letter into pieces and put them in the ashtray for the breeze to blow away. *All right,* I thought. *Okay.* For the rest of that morning I felt angry and betrayed and sad, and then by noon, after a long walk along the walls of the Fortezza, I felt better. And then I felt lightened, relieved and guilty at the same time, as if something had been decided for me, as if I'd gotten away with something I shouldn't have. *"She* did it," I murmured as I looked over the Fortezza to the blue-and-green-shuttered houses below. It was as if a door had unexpectedly opened, and I had ducked out of my past entirely, a clean getaway, with no one even knowing I had gone.

I didn't send Jena the letter about Governotou. Instead I fired back a postcard, yes, of the Venetian harbor. *I don't know what you want me to say,* I wrote. *I can't say anything more than what I can.* I mailed it, and breathed deeply. I smelled oleander and rhododendron, the oil-and-vegetable smell of the sea. I would write no more letters. I was free.

A BUS WHICH RAN along the coast stopped at Varka, about six kilometers from Governotou. From there I hired a taxi, and so arrived late one morning in the village. It was small: a taverna, a bakery, a *kafenion* shaded by a large plane tree. Harsh sunlight reflected off stone houses which squatted along narrow dirt streets, paths really. Other houses, scattered like pebbles on a beach, dotted the gorse-covered hills around and above the village. When my taxi stopped by the *kafenion,* children in underpants and T-shirts stared, than ran away. A woman in black walked by, carrying a basket of laundry. Somewhere, a shutter closed, then closed again. Goat bells.

Here is where Magnus had come, I thought. Maybe he had sat at this very *kafenion* and drunk a coffee or a beer before beginning the hike to the monastery.

Two old men, one potbellied, the other gnarled as his walking stick, watched balefully as I put my daypack on an outdoor table and sat down. Inside the *kafenion,* I could hear the rolling of dice, the clack of backgammon pieces. The children reappeared across the street. One boy raised a toy gun and fired at me, making an *ack-ack* sound. I raised my hand in imitation of a pistol, cocked my thumb, and fired back. They screamed and giggled. The boy boldly shot me again, shrieked, and disappeared with the others down the street.

A thin-faced young man with hair that flopped over his forehead came out of the *kafenion. "Ena nescafé,"* I said. He gave the slightest of nods and walked back inside. Fifteen minutes later—I was beginning to wonder if I'd been forgotten—the coffee was served, lukewarm.

"Do you speak English?" I asked the waiter.

"English, sure." He shifted his feet. Two men now appeared from the *kafenion.* One wore a thin knit cap, the other was bareheaded, bald except for a few wisps of hair, scraggly as the mountain gorse. They looked at me from behind the waiter, squinting slightly, as if not quite able to bring me in focus.

"Is there a monastery around here?" I asked. "In the mountains?"

The waiter crinkled his brow. He shook his head.

My heart sank. "No? No monastery?"

One of the men behind him mumbled something, and the waiter brushed him away with his fingers. "Say again," he asked. I realized he didn't understand much English at all.

"Mon-as-tery?" I said slowly.

The young man brightened. "Ah, *monastiri, monastiri!*" He turned to the men. *"Monastiri,"* he said triumphantly, and they nodded. He pointed down the street to a small church.

"No," I said, shaking my head. *"Monastiri.* There." I gestured to the hills around us. I struggled to find some simple word for "abandoned." *"Monastiri.* No people." The waiter looked puzzled. "Nobody there," I said.

Several men asked questions in rapid-fire Greek, to which the waiter replied in irritation, and then someone behind me said, "You want to know about monastery?" It was my taxi driver, still here. In our drive to Governotou, we hadn't talked at all, so I didn't know he spoke English. He tapped the young man on his head, as if it were a hollow drum. *"Monastiri, monastiri,"* he repeated. He looked at me. "He does not hear."

"Can you ask them if there's a monastery in the mountains?"

The driver translated and this time several heads nodded vigorously. One man pointed in the direction the children had disappeared. "In mountains, yes," my driver translated. "No one there. All gone."

"That's it," I said excitedly. "Ask them how I get there."

Again, the staccato of questions, gestures, replies. How, I wondered, had Magnus ever found it?

"Why do you want to go there? they ask. It is all gone." The driver made a scissoring motion with his hands, palms down. "Finish."

"I'm a writer," I said. He raised his brows. "I've heard that the monastery's a very interesting place."

"*Sinrafeos,*" he translated, and the men seemed to exhale slightly. One smiled, and wrote in the air. I shook my head and mimed typing.

"You write about Greece?" The driver swung his arms around, as if all Greece came under his protection.

"Yes," I lied.

"You will write about me?" He pressed his hand to his chest, almost shyly.

"Sure." I grinned.

He laughed and said something to the others, and they laughed too. A man with a black mustache cocked his head and raised his chin, as if posing for on old-fashioned photograph. And then all of them were talking at once. The driver puckered his lips. "There is a path, they say." He pointed to the waiter. "He will show you."

"Far?" I asked. "Many kilometers?"

It was the waiter who answered. "Not so far." He tapped his watch. "Not an hour, I think."

As we left, the driver called to me, "You don't forget. You write about me." I waved.

The waiter and I walked through dirt streets, beside whitewashed houses shaded by olive, lemon, and plane trees. In only a few minutes we were ascending a narrow switchback path—a goat path, really—that wound around the flank of a scree-covered hill. Once we were around the curve, the village dropped from sight, and the morning seemed to become more silent. I was worried that my guide was going to accompany me the whole way, which was not what I wanted at all. I was wondering what to do when he stopped and pointed. "There," he said. The path split in two—one fork continuing around the hill, the other beginning a steep descent. "You go"—he pointed to the second path and made a gesture, as if I should take wing and fly—"there."

"I can't get lost? Just stay on the path?"

He looked at me blankly. "There, *there.*" He mimed a fast quickstep. "No problem."

I hitched my backpack and started down the path. The sun was just past noon and very hot, and I readjusted the bandana around my neck. A lizard darted across the path. I looked back and waved to the young man, who stood watching me with crossed arms. When I looked back again, he was gone.

The path cut almost immediately into shadow, and the landscape changed. Scrub trees and Cretan pine grew more thickly here, and the opposite mountainside was green and purplish with gorse and heath. I could smell sage and thyme everywhere. In the distance I heard roosters crowing from Governotou, or some other village. Cicadas. The only other sound was the crunching of my shoes along the path. Occasionally I'd dislodge a pebble, and it would skitter over the edge of the path and down the hillside into the gorge. I was totally and wondrously alone.

Maybe I *would* write about this, I thought. I would re-create everything: the cab ride, the village and the old men, the butterflies that rose like small winged ghosts from the scrub as I walked by, the clouds scudding through a sea-sky. And I thought how strange life was, that I was here, walking along a hot path on a Cretan mountainside, half a world and a thousand years from Philadelphia, my family, Jena. They seemed to belong to another life, one whose claims of expectation and duty were fast fading. I was overwhelmed by a feeling, like a dry, warm shiver, that the only thing that mattered was to be here, free, filling my lungs with the fragrant, bone-dry Cretan air. Anything was possible, if only I imagined, then dared it. One pursued something, and one found it, as I would find the monastery, the room and its blue wooden table, the dried flowers, the bowl and the coins. And after I'd seen everything, I would follow the river to the sea, strip naked, and swim, and all I had ever been would be washed away, leaving me naked and cleansed in my new life.

I sat on a rock, took the mineral water from my pack, and drank. I looked at my watch. I'd been walking for almost three-quarters of an hour: I must almost be there. I was putting the bottle back in my pack when I heard a voice. At first I thought it was somebody calling somebody else across the ravine, but then I heard more clearly.

"American. Hey, American."

I looked up the path, shading my eyes from the sun. Someone—a man—was running down the path. For a moment I was afraid I'd forgotten to pay at the *kafenion,* or was on the wrong trail and he had come all this way to tell me. I waited as he chuffed toward me.

"American," he panted. "Hey." He raised his hand in a salute. He was short and wiry, with a thin black mustache and thinning black hair beneath his corduroy cap, which he'd been holding as he ran so it wouldn't fall off. He was perspiring heavily—he must have run much of the way from the village. I could smell the harsh tobacco emanating from his clothes. "You go—to monastery?" he asked.

Offering himself as a guide, I thought with dismay.

"I don't need a guide," I said. "I just want to look around by myself."

He seemed puzzled.

"No guide," I said.

He brightened, understanding. "No, no. No guide." He giggled, and shook his head. "No guide." And then: "You are writer?"

So they'd told him that, too. "Yes," I said.

He beamed, as if this were the greatest news he'd ever heard. I thought he might clap his hands. "I show you something. You must see. I come to show you."

"Show me what?"

He shook his head. "I cannot tell you. A"—he searched for the word—"surprise. You are writer. You must see."

"See what?"

He shook his head again, more slowly. "It is important."

"I'm going to the monastery," I said. And then louder, as if he were hard of hearing, "The *monastery.*"

He made a dismissive gesture. "Monastery—nothing there, nothing, nothing." He spat. "What I show you—very important." He lowered his voice. "For your writing."

"But what *is* it?"

He twirled his hand, as if spinning the air into taffy. "It is wonderful. You will see. Come." He started back up the path, saw my hesitation, and said, "You will go to monastery after. Yes. After."

Who was he? Why wouldn't he just say what he wanted me to see? Indeed, in all this barrenness, what could there possibly *be* to show me? I had never been good at dismissing people. Here, in all this empty landscape, I felt trapped.

"You *are* writer?" He looked at me intently, as if he might have made a mistake.

And now I could almost hear Bitters mocking me: *And you didn't go? He was probably going to take you to his beautiful goatherd daughter for much loving. A wonderful story! But you missed it.*

You have to be there, Magnus had said. *You have to be ready.*

"Okay," I said. "I'll go."

He broke into a wide grin. "Okay," he said. "Okay. Okay." We started back up the path. He was almost bouncing with delight.

Maybe it will *be an adventure,* I thought, and already imagined myself back at the Odos, telling Bitters, *Before going to the monastery, I met the strangest little man who showed me . . .* And now I could imagine possibilities: a wonderful view of the gorge, a ruin of some sort, a cave . . .

Every now and then the man glanced over his shoulder to see how I was keeping up. It seemed incredible he could walk so briskly after running so far to catch up with me. Was he afraid that if we stopped, or slowed down, I might change my mind? About a quarter-mile back up the path, he stepped off it, and went down an even narrower one I hadn't noticed before.

"Where are we going?" I called. He turned and waved, and briskly marched on. He was amazingly nimble on the narrow path. *He must be half-goat,* I thought.

I looked as far as I could, but couldn't see where the path led.

And I thought: *What if he has nothing to show me?* What if he were slightly mad, the village idiot, maybe, and I was being led on a wild-goose chase?

Or—other possibility—what if he were just trying to lure me *away* from the monastery? Was there something there I wasn't supposed to see? Contraband? Stolen goods cached there to be taken downriver to the sea?

That's crazy, I told myself.

Yet the farther we descended into the shadows of the gorge, the more anxious I grew. There was nothing around here, nothing at all.

He is luring me somewhere, I thought. To rob me? Is that why he wanted me off the main path?

Easy, I told myself. If he wanted to rob me, he could've done it already. Who, after all, was around to see? I was imagining things, I—

I felt something cold in my stomach. *What if he wanted not just to rob, but to kill me?* His jacket could easily conceal a knife, one of those wicked two-bladed ones the mountain goatherds used which I'd seen in the shops in Réthimnon. And wouldn't killing me be more likely, after all? A simple robbery—they would soon know, and know him—back at the village. Yes, I would have to be killed.

Fear, harsh and acidic, rose in my throat. *No*, I told myself, *this is crazy.* If he wanted to kill me, he could already have done it. We were already well out of sight of the path above. Why go farther?

Because he had to dispose of my body. Perhaps he knew a place where he could hide it—a cave, a gully—and that's where we were going. He would hide my body where it wouldn't be found right away, if ever. Why drag or carry it when I could be lured there?

And now I regretted everything—having followed this man, having come to Governotou, having come to Crete at all. It had been foolish, foolish, foolish, vanity and delusion. I could see my father and my mother and Jena looking at me with sad, knowing eyes: *See what comes of this, of your trying to leave us? Too late, too late now.* And it was. I'd gone too far down this path. If I turned and ran, he would pursue me, run me down. He was faster, stronger maybe, and he had a weapon. My death would only come sooner.

"I want to know where we're going," I cried.

"Only a little now." He held his thumb and forefinger an inch apart, as if time could be measured so. "Very soon. You will see." Perhaps he sensed my nervousness, for he made a beckoning gesture, almost gentle, as if I were a reluctant child. "Come," he said. "For your book."

Numbly I stumbled on.

The path broke into a clearing. The man stopped. "There . . ."

Not more than thirty yards away, nestled between two undulations of the hillside, was a small cottage of whitewashed stone, its windows shuttered. It was like any you might encounter on a trail in Greece. It might even have been a chapel—you often found them in out-of-the-way places, built by some patron in hopes of salvation for his good works.

"What's in there?" I asked.

He grinned and wigwagged his hand. "Come—you will see."

I didn't move. We were some fifteen yards apart. My throat was dry, my heart hammering.

He looked puzzled. "Come," he coaxed. And took a step toward me.

I ran. I ran in fear and I ran in panic and I ran gasping, my lungs unable to take in enough hot, burning air. I ran with my hands as much as my legs, almost swimming, and I ran only once looking back, to see him not pursuing me at all, just watching, both arms extended, palms outward, as if in entreaty, or benediction. I ran back to the main path and stood there wheezing like an old man, and then I stumbled and ran again. I ran until I was back in the village, and only then did I stop running. My lungs ached, and my stomach heaved. A woman stuck her head out of a window and looked at me. Embarrassed, I turned away, and walked toward the road and the *kafenion*. The men were still sitting under the plane tree, children were still darting up and down the streets.

My taxi driver was there too, a glass of brandy and two

espresso cups before him. "Hey, American!" He waved cheerily.
I walked over. My shirt was soaked, my throat dry and raw.

"You have been to monastery? So fast?"

I nodded. I took my mineral water from the knapsack and
drank. The old men were looking at me. Could they sense my
recent panic? Did it show so easily?

"I wait for you," my driver said. "I know you will want
ride back."

"Yes," I said. I put the empty bottle on the table.

"So," he asked expansively, "how was monastery?"

"Nothing. Just old stones."

He laughed.

ON THE DRIVE BACK, I told Stavros—he finally introduced
himself, and we shook hands awkwardly across the seat—that I'd
encountered a strange man on the trail.

"He had me follow him to a little house. He wanted to
show me something."

Stavros tapped the side of his head. "Crazy."

"What could he have meant?"

Stavros shrugged.

How foolish to be asking him, I thought. If I wanted to
know, shouldn't I have asked at the village? And then I wondered: Why hadn't I? Had I been in such a hurry to leave?

I settled back in the seat. The blinding, noonday fear that
I'd felt on the path seemed more and more irrational, and I felt
ashamed. I imagined my strange guide—totally harmless, after
all—telling the men at the *kafenion* about my flight, and all of
them shrugging their shoulders and tapping their heads and
laughing.

He had, after all, only wanted to show me something—
and I had run away. I tried to excuse myself: his secrecy, his

strange laughter, the harshness of the landscape, the shiftings of clouds and light and shadow that had dogged the day. But still, it came back to one thing: I had run away.

The drive lulled me, and my thoughts drifted. I tried to imagine what was in that little cottage that he so desperately wanted to show me. I imagined everything, the possibilities growing more fanciful: a prize goat, pictures of relatives in America, relics of Saint John the Stranger, treasures from the monastery that he'd found and hoarded.

Or maybe it was *someone* he wanted me to see. A hermit monk? His wife, who wanted to meet an American? An aged uncle who'd once lived in Chicago? His goatherd daughter? At one point—I must have dozed—I saw him opening the door, and behind it, smiling at me, her legs crossed almost daintily, was Magnus's Danish girl. *See*, the man said, *she was here all the time, waiting for you.*

I sighed and shifted in my seat.

Back in Réthimnon, I walked around furtively, like a ghost, and indeed, people seemed to look through me and around me as if I really were one. I couldn't bear to go to the Odos and see Bitters, nor anyone else who might have stories to tell.

I would leave Crete soon, I knew. I was no writer, no adventurer. I could see my father shaking his head as if to say, *I told you so,* and I thought bitterly, *All right, I give up. You got me.*

I would marry Jena. I knew this with both hope and resignation. Perhaps I wasn't ready, perhaps we weren't even right for one another. But at least she would never scare me.

In the middle of my last night on Crete, before I left on the morning ferry to Piraeus and the plane back home, I awoke suddenly feeling I knew who was behind the door of that little house. It was an old woman sitting alone in the cool darkness. She is alone, she is withered, she is wearing one of those heavy black dresses that every Greek woman over sixty seems to wear. She is staring at the table, as if something very small and fine—a breadcrumb, an insect—is there. Whatever it is commands her utmost, if unneeded, concentration. Why is she staring so? Why is it so dark? Why are there no candles? And then I realize she is blind.

The old woman, somehow, is me.

But all that was later. In the taxi with Stavros, I still felt only shame and the metallic aftertaste of fear. And something else, like a black wave, a dark swell come to carry me off, down, away from Governotou and Crete. It was all the rest of my life, come to claim me.

"I wish I knew what it was he wanted to show me," I said again, as if this time Stavros could really tell me.

"What does it matter?" he said. "You saw what you came for, didn't you?" He waved his hand. "You saw Governotou very well."

Part II

SKATING IN

THE DARK

Skating in the Dark

—*January 1972*

Northern *Pennsylvania,* forest land, near the New York
border. The coldest winter in a decade. Every day seems to break
a record, the weatherman solemnly reports, and the local newspaper's headline reads, "Baby, It's Cold!" People stamp their
feet in stores and gas stations and make jokes and small talk
which hang in the air like icicles. The lake froze in late November. In December it snowed and snowed, and the snow remains,
not just because it's cold, but also because only summer houses,
empty now, surround the lake. They lay scrunched up for the
winter, snow-capped, tight-lipped, tidy. No people shovel their
drives, no children make snowmen and snow angels in the yards,
so the snow stays clear and icy, tracked only by squirrels and
rabbits and the occasional deer which, hunting season over,
walks through the yards like an old senator.

Frank and Jena are driving up the lake road to his parents' summer house. They've been married for three years, and live in Southern California now. Frank is a technical writer for a firm that makes navigational parts for airplanes—"what's inside the black boxes," he tells people, who ask no more, for which he's grateful. Jena is a curriculum consultant for the El Monte school system. They've been visiting Frank's parents in Tyler, part of what's becoming, Frank realizes, an annual holiday swing back East—Christmas with one set of parents, New Year's with the other. The inevitability of this vacation and those in the years to come, made even more so if they have children, depresses Frank. Neither set of parents seems to have any desire to visit them in Southern California, not even in winter. "I'm too old for Disneyland," his mother tells him, although Frank feels she would really like to go, if only his father could be convinced. "I couldn't take all that flatness," his father says, and clucks disapprovingly, as if geography were somehow culpable. No matter that Frank has told him again and again that there are mountains galore where they live, ticking them off—the San Bernardinos, the San Gabriels, the Sierras—their names churchly and eternal. His father nods impatiently. His inability to believe in these mountains, Frank feels, is somehow a lack of faith in him.

On a whim, after leaving his parents this morning to drive to an inn near Toronto where they will spend the weekend, they've taken a detour to the summer house. When Frank mentioned that they were passing within fifteen miles of it, Jena had been astonished.

"I didn't know your folks had a summer place," she said.

"They got it when I was ten. An uncle of my mother's died and left us some money. Mom and I'd go there for a month in the summer, and Dad would come up on weekends. The rest of the summer we'd rent it out."

Jena had insisted they go see it, even though Frank was reluctant. "I don't understand why you're not more curious to see it," she said.

He isn't. Like Tyler, it is part of the past, and the past is a place he doesn't like to visit. In the past, it is always winter.

Every so often the car skirrs and slides on the hard-packed snow which covers what is, in better season, a dirt road. Frank thinks the house might be difficult to find, but surprisingly, it's not. Like a groundhog returning to its den, he turns up one road and down another, and yes, there it is, capped with snow, its clapboards lightly frosted. Except for a different trim color, a little more sag to the sides, it's the same.

"Well, there it is," Frank says. He lets the engine idle.

Jena studies it. "It's cute," she says finally. She smiles. "You know, I always wanted to have a summer house when I was a kid. All those books I read—all those English ladies always had country houses. It seemed so sophisticated."

"But you *lived* in the country, Jen."

"It's not the same thing. Where you live is never the *real* country. In the real country, people play badminton and croquet. They follow the hounds."

"Well, that's not this place," Frank says. "This is just a little dumpy summer house."

"Can we get in?"

Frank debates with himself a moment, then says, "There used to be a key under the porch. We'd leave it for the guy who checked up on things over the winter."

They park the car by the side of the road, as close as Frank deems safe. The drifts are up to their knees, the crusted snow like a tough scab, the softer snow beneath, granular and icy. They work their way to the porch in back. Here the ground slopes to a small dock and the lake, frozen a gray-blue with darker black patches freckled through it. On the beach side and toward the middle, a few people are skating.

Frank kicks away snow and ducks under the porch. He gropes along the studs for the key.

"Find it?" Jena calls.

"It's *dark* under here."

"Want me to get the flashlight?" Without waiting for a reply, she backtracks through the snow to the car. Frank feels along the timbers, his hands brushing cobwebs. When she comes back, he tells her he doesn't think there's any key.

She hands him the flashlight. "Why don't you look anyway?"

"Jena, believe me."

"Okay, *I'll* look." She flicks on the flashlight, brushes past him, and stoops under the porch. Frank sighs and stares at the lake. Down from the public beach, the houses dwindle, like a series of dots, disappearing into the uncut forest of pine and spruce that rims the lake.

Jena pops out. "No key."

"Told you."

They go up the porch steps. The curtains are drawn over the windows. Jena rattles one, then another. "I wish we could get in," she says.

"It's not much, really, Jena. It's just a little summer place."

She's down the steps again and tramping around the side. She rattles the kitchen window, shoves it. Frank follows. He wants to be gone—it's cold, and the sky is getting grayer.

"Frank." Jena's eyes crinkle mischievously. "Let's break in."

"What?"

"It'd be easy to do, wouldn't it?" She rattles the window again. "I think the jamb on this one is loose. We could . . ." She shoves up hard on the window. "I think—if I can just jam a piece of wood or something under here—I can jimmy it up."

"Jen, come on! We could get arrested."

"It's your place, Frank. Nobody can arrest you for breaking into your own place, right?" She shoves again. The latch falls off and clatters between the panes. The window creaks, then gives.

"You've busted it!" Frank says in dismay. But already Jena has her hands on the sill. With a grunt, she hikes herself up, swings one leg over, and disappears into the darkness of the house. Frank is disturbed: it shouldn't be this easy to break in. Jena reappears, grinning naughtily. "C'mon," she whispers. Before lifting himself up, Frank glances around, as if someone might be watching, ready to emerge from the woods, stern and wraithlike, to point an accusing finger and demand an apology. He hikes himself up and in. The window is above the sink. Frank slides into it, then jumps down onto the floor. Jena is standing with her arms crossed, still grinning.

"This is great, Jena." Frank turns the broken latch in his fingers. "Now I'm going to have to *fix* this."

"I'll do it," she says. "The screws came out, is all. It's no big deal."

The house smells faintly like creosote, musty and stale. Dead insects, trapped inside when the house was closed up in the fall, lie like dark crumbs on the sink top, on the floor. Jena flicks the light switch, but nothing happens.

"You didn't really expect the electricity to be on, did you?" Frank asks.

"Don't be a smart-ass." She walks to the front room, and Frank follows. A thin layer of dust coats the furniture. *Where, he wonders, does dust come from, when everything is shut so tight?*

"So?" she asks. "How's it seem?"

"The same. Same furniture, everything. Just a little older." The print of *Lake Leman by Moonlight* still hangs in its cracked glass frame over the fireplace, and the ugly driftwood lamp, a purchase from a childhood trip to Florida, still adorns the end table. Frank lifts it to show Jena. "You know, when I was a kid I used to think worms lived in this wood. I'd stare and stare at the holes, waiting for them to come out."

She laughs.

"I don't know where I got that idea." He puts the lamp back on the table.

Jena goes upstairs. Frank can hear the floorboards creak and groan, as if the house is protesting these people who've disturbed its rest. He opens the shades; the dulled afternoon light only seems to make things gloomier.

Jena reappears at the top of the stairs. "Frank," she yells. "There's quilts and sheets and things in the closet up here!"

"So?"

"You know what I think would be great?" She's down the stairs, taking the last two with a little hop. "Wouldn't it be great to stay here tonight?"

"Jena, are you nuts?"

"It'd be fun!"

"There's no heat, no lights—"

"We can build a fire! I saw the wood outside. We can get some beer and marshmallows and hot dogs and roast them."

He shakes his head, half-smiling.

"We'd be all alone. Snowbound." She arches her brows suggestively. "We can pile a bunch of quilts on the bed and snuggle in."

"Sure—and freeze to death."

"There's the fire. And look." She points to the corner. Frank sees the portable kerosene heater his parents used for chilly summer evenings.

"Probably no fuel for it, Jen."

"Let's at least look, Frank. Come on." She squeezes his hand. "It'll be romantic. We could use a little more romance in our lives."

"Jena, we guaranteed the reservations at the inn!"

She looks at her watch. "We can still call and cancel. Tell them we're coming tomorrow." She goes to the porch door and pulls. It doesn't open.

"Deadbolt, Jen. We'd have to go in and out the window."

She looks at him entreatingly. "Honey, let's just stay and have a good time, okay? It'll be an adventure."

Frank sighs. He looks out the front window. Already the far shore is in darkness, trees blending with clouds and sky and lake in a swab of indigo. Jena rests her chin on his shoulder. "Wouldn't this be a wonderful place to bring kids?" she says softly.

"I suppose." Frank remembers a line from a poem in college—Blake, he thinks—in which children are trudging home at dusk: *No light is seen on the darkening green.* Or something like that. There are no lights on here, nor in any other house, and the lake is blackening like a spreading stain. Spookily, as if echoing his thought, Jena murmurs, "Just us." But she says it with pleasure, whereas all it seems to him is that they are indeed alone.

She rubs his arms. "Gonna have a good time?"

"Sure." He kisses her lightly. *Romance,* he thinks. *Okay.*

"Well, I'm hungry," Jena says. "Do you want to build a fire and I'll cook?"

Frank spreads his hands. "Cook what?"

"We'll get some stuff at that store down at the cutoff. We can call the inn from there, too."

"Jen, look—let's not overdo this. If we're staying here,

let's at least go out to eat. There's a restaurant down the road."
He doesn't know this, but assumes there must be one.

She's suspicious. "You think that if we go away from here,
then I won't want to come back."

"No, I—"

"*I'll* go get the stuff. I'll call the inn."

"Hey, I don't want you driving down that road in the
dark."

"Okay. So you go, then." Jena plops down on the sofa.
"I'll start the fire."

Frank sighs.

"If you get some kerosene, too," she says, "maybe we can
get that heater working."

"Absolutely. Kerosene."

Jena cocks her head. "You know, this really could be a lot
of fun."

Frank holds up his hands in a gesture of surrender. "I'm
off."

THE CAR SLIPS and slides as he drives down the road. It is
almost dark, and Frank is amazed, as he was as a child, how
quickly day can vanish in this season. A blink and a flash, and
the dark is there again, like a mean trick. Maybe because the
day's sunlight is so intense, night in Southern California seems
more like an interlude, a pause between sunshines. Here, it
prevails.

Frank is still irritated by their change of plans, but tells
himself he shouldn't be. They are there for the night, okay.
Make the best of it.

Duchene's is still Duchene's, which is reassuring, although the store is larger, the old clapboard front bricked over
and a small cupola added in imitation of a colonial posthouse.

Inside, the wooden floors are tiled over, the bare bulbs which were strung across the ceiling and which always reminded him of carnivals replaced now by fluorescents.

Frank buys hot dogs, buns, marshmallows, potatoes for baking. He buys beer. At least they won't need a refrigerator to keep it cold. *We're going to freeze tonight,* he thinks. *Freeze, freeze, freeze.* He remembers kerosene for the heater. He's at the checkout counter when he remembers ketchup and mustard. And since there's no water to wash with, they'll need plastic knives and forks and spoons. Plates. Jesus, it didn't end. To have one simple meal, you needed everything. He's at the counter again when he thinks of something else: as a goodwill gesture, he buys a pan of self-popping popcorn. Frank smiles as he thinks how pleased Jena will be.

"I used to come here all the time when I was a kid," he says to the cashier, a heavyset girl who stares at him from behind thick glasses. She rings up his purchases and starts stuffing them in paper bags. "Does Mr. Duchene still own the place?"

"It's his name on the store."

"You know him?"

She shakes her head. "I work evenings. I don't see nobody. Some woman hired me, but I hear she went to Buffalo for an operation awhile back."

"I used to buy candy here. Baseball cards, marbles— everything. I spent a lot of hours in this place."

"Well, I do too." She pushes the bags of groceries across the counter.

Frank is halfway down the road before he remembers that he hasn't called the inn. He curses, slows down. There are no cleared drives in which to turn. He stops and backs up to turn on the road. When he tries going forward, the rear wheels slip and skirr—an ice slick, or a soft spot. He lets the car roll back a little—and feels it slide. He quickly jams the car in forward and accelerates, but it's too late, the right rear wheel spins frantically, slides even farther back. He's off the road.

"Goddammit!" Frank smacks the steering wheel. He opens the glove compartment for the flashlight, but it's not there, of course, it's back at the house. He gets out. There's no moon, everything is pitch-dark, but he can tell by the cant of the car that he's going nowhere. Frank pounds his fist, once, twice, on the car, as if it were a tiring beast that could be exhorted to one more effort. "I can't *believe* this," he mutters.

Now what? He is halfway between the store and the house. He can walk a mile back to Duchene's and call a tow, though God knows who he could get to come out this evening. And even then—what? He just might get stuck again before they got away in the morning. The road looks equally dark in either direction. He is cold and he is hungry. Frank decides to walk to the house: in the morning they can call the tow, be pulled up and out and ready to go. The car's far enough over to the side that it doesn't pose any real danger, and besides, who would be driving down this road tonight anyway? "Only crazy people," he says to the dark. He gets the grocery bags, locks the car, and trudges up the road.

WHEN HE ARRIVES back at the house, there's light in the living room—how is that possible? He stomps up the porch steps and, both arms full with the bags, kicks the door. He is in a foul, foul mood.

"Frank?" He hears her muted voice through the door.

"It's goddam Kriss Kringle. Open up."

"Locked, remember?"

It's the capper on all the frustrations of the day. Frank clomps down the steps and around to the kitchen window. Jena opens it and shines the flashlight on him.

"What took you so long? I was worried."

"The goddam car's stuck." He hands her the bags. "I had to *walk* back."

"How'd it get stuck?"

He pushes himself up and through. "Jesus, it is *dark* out there. No moon, no nothing. It was like the goddam Russian steppes. I thought I heard wolves howling." He takes off his gloves and rubs his hands. "I never realized how uphill that road is."

"But how'd it happen?"

"I was trying to turn around to call the goddam inn! Which I didn't do, by the way, so there goes our deposit. I just can't *believe* all this! Just because you—"

"Hey, come on." She raises her hand in protest. "It's not my fault you got stuck."

"I want a beer." Frank rummages in the bag and pulls out the six-pack. "Jesus, I thought I was going to get eaten by wolves." Jena giggles. "It's not *funny.* I heard rustlings. There are things out there."

"Popcorn!" Jena cries with delight, pulling it from the bag. "And *beans!* Honey, you did great." She puts her hands on his shoulders. "Here, come on. I'll give you a back rub."

"I don't *want* a back rub. I want to eat. I want to get warm."

Jena makes a beckoning, flirtatious gesture. "Come in the front room. The fire's going really nice." She grasps his hand.

It does seem almost toasty. The fire is crackling brightly, the smell of creosote and must is gone. Two oil lanterns illuminate the room.

"I found them," Jena says proudly. "They were in the pantry. Full of oil, luckily."

In spite of himself, Frank feels better. He takes off his boots and parka and sits close to the fire.

"You just sit right here," Jena says. "I'll get something to cook the hot dogs with. I'll take care of it all." She goes into the kitchen and comes back with a cooking fork. She spears three hot dogs on the tines, puts the potatoes to bake in a corner of the fireplace. Her reddish-blond hair glows in the light. She leans over and kisses him. "Still friends?"

"Sure," he says, not looking at her.

"Gonna have a good time?"

He waves his hand. Sure. Why not?

WHILE JENA COOKS the hot dogs, Frank tries to start the kerosene heater. The directions on the side are long worn away, and he can't remember how his father used to do it. He fiddles with the stopcock, twists valves, turns the pilot on and off. He applies match after match. It won't light.

"Here, let me try," Jena says.

"What makes you think you can do this any better, Jen? I mean, have you ever even seen one of these before?"

"Hey, I just thought I'd try. You're not having very much luck."

He gets up. "Be my guest."

She hands the hot dogs to Frank and kneels beside the heater. He goes over to the fire, stokes the coals, and tests the potatoes with a fork. Hard as a brick. With luck, he thinks, they'll be ready for breakfast. At least the hot dogs are almost done. He puts some buns on to warm. He hears a hiss, and a whoosh.

"There!" Jena says. "It's going."

He's astonished. "What the hell did you do?"

"You just had to"—she points—"press the reset button."

"I never even *saw* that."

She looks at him with a bemused smile. "How are you ever going to teach our kids anything practical?"

Frank turns over a bun. "I'll teach them other things."

"Like what?"

"Spiritual things. Matters of the heart."

"You're an expert in that, huh?"

Frank looks to see how she means this, but can't tell. His wife's face is as blank as snow.

"Maybe we won't have any kids," he says.

Jena blinks, as if she really didn't hear this and will let it pass, wind over grass. She comes back to the fire, squats, takes the hot dogs off the fork, and puts them in the buns. "I forget. Did you get mustard?"

Frank nods. Jena extracts the mustard from the bag, twists off the top. "Do you want some?"

"Sure."

She spreads it on the hot dog, but doesn't hand it to him yet, just holds it. "Frank, I just wanted to get the goddam thing *working,*" she says. "That's all."

He takes the hot dog from her, puts it down, and puts his arm around her. He feels her tense slightly before letting him hold her. Despite their proximity to the fire, she seems cold, and Frank shivers, too. "I'm sorry," he says. "I don't know why I'm in such a bad mood."

She doesn't reply. Staring into the fire, Frank has a vision of them frozen in their bed, arms wrapped tight around each other in a cold, locked embrace, as if to squeeze from their bodies the last bit of warmth, the last vital breath. Their eyes are open, watching each other to the end. *They look so lifelike,* the people who find them say. But they are frozen, and they are dead.

LATER, AFTER hot dogs and half-baked potatoes and cole slaw and a few beers, Frank is feeling better. The kerosene heater has warmed the room considerably, and the fire and lanterns have given it a cheery glow. He and Jena can take heater and lanterns upstairs tonight, and with the quilts, she may be right, it might actually be cozy. He lets his fingers travel down Jena's back. "Mmmm," she says, and rests her head on her knees. In the morning, Frank thinks, he'll walk down to Duchene's and get their car pulled out. No—they'll *both* walk there—no sense getting stuck again turning around at the house. And then they'll go. *Our adventure,* he thinks.

"I'll go make the bed," Jena says. "You stay here and keep cozy."

He's just thrown the paper plates into the fire when Jena comes back down. "Look." She holds up two pairs of ice skates.

"Where'd you find *those?*"

"In the closet in the hall. Did you guys go skating in the summer, or what?"

"I don't know where they came from. I've never seen them before." Frank inspects the skates—a man's and a woman's pair, the leather old but cared for, oiled, the laces new, the blades recently sharpened. "They must be Mom and Dad's. I know they come up in the winter sometimes, but I never thought they skated."

"Maybe they belong to friends of theirs." Jena's already trying on the lady's pair. She shakes her foot, wiggles her ankle. "My God, they fit! A little tight, but they fit." She nods toward the other pair. "Try them on, honey."

"For God's sake, why?"

She jerks her thumb toward the lake. "We can go skating!"

"You're kidding."

"No. Really."

"Jena, are you crazy? It's cold! It's goddam *night* out there."

Still on skates, she clomps over to the window and lifts

the shade. "No moon. That makes it all the neater."

"Besides—the skates probably don't even fit."

"Well, try them on. See."

"Jena, I don't *want* to go skating. I'm just getting comfortable here."

"Frank, it's like we were *meant* to be here. To find those skates. Come on."

"So you go skate. I'll stay here."

"Where's your sense of adventure?"

"I wish you'd stop asking me that, Jena. That's really beginning to irritate me."

She crosses her arms. "You know, you used to be a lot more fun. You're becoming a real stick-in-the-mud as you get older. Just like your father."

He waves.

"Okay," she says. "I'll go." She puts on her muffler and parka and cap.

"I'm not a stick-in-the-mud," he says.

Jena makes a chuffing sound, whether of acceptance or disdain he can't tell. Frank follows her into the kitchen. When she's at the window, he asks, "How do you know where to go?"

"What do you mean? I walk down to the lake. What's so hard?"

"It's *dark*, Jena. There're bushes and things along the bank. You don't just walk out onto the ice."

"I'll take the flashlight." She clomps across the room and gets it from the table. When she's at the window again, Frank says, "Hold on."

She turns and stares at him impassively.

"I'll come," he says.

"I thought you didn't want to."

"You can't be out there at night by yourself."

She laughs. "Don't be silly. What's going to happen?"

"What if the ice breaks and you fall in?"

"They were skating out there this afternoon. I think it's okay."

"You can't always tell. There're . . . patches where the ice is thinner. Because of lake currents." He doesn't know if this is true or not. But it sounds right.

She breaks into a grin. "Honey, I'll be skating so fast, I'll just go right over them."

He sees her skating over infinite space and infinite depths, her blades barely touching the ice which has no time to feel her weight, she is there, she is gone. She disappears into the blackness of night and the wind.

"Besides," Jena says, "maybe *you'll* fall in and I'll have to fish *you* out. Maybe you better stay here. You'll be in a lot better spirits if you do."

He shakes his head. "I'm going. You shouldn't be out there by yourself."

Jena is looking at him warily. "You really don't have to do this."

"I know." Frank puts on a skate. The fit is a little loose, but if he wears a second pair of wool socks, they should almost fit. *Oh why bother?* he thinks. He doesn't really need them.

"You're going to blame me later, aren't you?" Jena says. "You're going to get grumpy."

"No," he says. "Come on. You want to skate. Let's go skate."

They go out the window and tromp down the slope toward the lake. The frigid air stings his lungs. The snow is quickly up to his knees. "You're so goddam stubborn," Jena says, stumbling behind him.

And then they're at the dock, and he sees he was wrong,

it's easy to get out onto the lake after all, the drifts having created, in effect, a ramp down. They're soon out on the ice. It seems darker here than it could ever possibly be. There is no moon, no stars, and the clouds seem to have descended over the lake in a black, vaporous fog. He and Jena stroke together, panting lightly, and Frank is amazed he's skating, that only his will, his legs, and the thin blades propel him. His legs strain with the unaccustomed motion, and his ankles wobble. He glances back at the house. To his surprise, it appears empty and dark, the light from the fire hardly visible. A little farther from shore and it disappears, and then the shoreline does too, dissolved by darkness, so that it is impossible to tell where the black of sky and earth meet. He can see only a few yards ahead, as if the ice were an extension of the sky, the perfect fulfillment of its black-ness. Soon he's puffing hard. In Southern California he runs about three times a week, but it seems to mean nothing now, whereas Jena, who hardly exercises at all, has already settled into a rhythm of quiet exhalations. They skate without talking to-ward what he thinks should be the middle of the lake.

"Hold on!" They stop while he catches his breath.

"Isn't this wild?" Jena's voice is flushed, excited.

"Real . . . dark . . . " he pants.

"It's like being in space! You can't tell where you're going."

"Great . . ."

"Come on," Jena says. "Take a chance." Before he can say anything more, she pushes off and away.

Frank bends over his knees and breathes deeply, again and again. He straightens up. "Jena?" She doesn't reply. He can see nothing through the darkness, which has thickened, become almost palpable. He listens, but can't hear her skates. Frank starts to skate, then stops. Which way did she go?

"Jena!"

There is no response from any direction.

He skates a few yards more, and stops again. Could something have happened to her? No, impossible. She skated off only a few minutes ago. He's heard no ice cracking, no cry. She either doesn't hear him, or is playing some game.

Why didn't she wait for me? he wonders. *Why did she just skate away?*

"Jena!"

No longer sure where he wants to go, Frank pushes off and almost immediately stumbles over something, an undulation or warp in the ice. He falls hard, and feels his ankle twist. He gets up and gingerly tests it. He grimaces. It *is* twisted. *I should've worn that second pair of socks,* Frank thinks. His wrist hurts, too—he must have landed on it in breaking his fall. *Great,* he thinks. He's out in the middle of the lake, not even sure which direction the house is in. The wind is gusting harder, passing by in long, sad exhalations. Frank hears the trees shaking like ratchets. Everywhere the black band of shoreline looks the same.

"Jena?" he yells. "Jena, I hurt my ankle!" But his words are like stones thrown into a pool so deep that the splash is immediately absorbed, and he realizes that words mean nothing here, they are not heard, let alone answered. Jena is gone, he is alone. It is the dark which now attends him.

And he hears something else, sharp and splintery. *The ice is groaning,* he thinks. He tells himself it's normal, ice makes these sounds, but still—had it been making them before? He listens. It seems louder, coming from all around him now. The lake is breaking beneath him! He can almost feel it cracking, yielding, not just here, but everywhere. Only ice, thin and treacherous, holds him. *Ice,* he thinks. *Water.* He will fall through, he will plunge into endless cold and blackness. Panicked, Frank pushes off, in what direction he doesn't know. His legs are wooden, he cannot push them, and his ankle throbs, but he can't stop or he will surely fall, *only water holds him.* The whole lake is groaning now, as if trying to cast off some great pain. Frank wants to cry out, but can't—his breath comes in short quick gasps, and besides, it would be futile, there is no one to hear, Jena is gone, she has left him, and the lake is not listening at all.

And then he's falling again, splayed and sliding on the ice, tripped over what he doesn't know, his own panic, perhaps. His face is so close to the ice that he can smell its faint redolence of muck and mulching leaves. And suddenly it seems the ice opens to him, not physically, but in luminescence, he can see into it, and staring up at him through the ice, mouth and eyes frozen wide, hands curled as if trying to break through the blacked surface, is a man's face. Frank shrieks and pushes to his feet. He tries to clomp-run, slips, and regains his balance. His ankle is throbbing, and his eyes tear in frustration and fear. And then he sees through the brume a shape—pilings, someone's dock. He's only twenty yards from shore! Frank almost cries with relief. He skates painfully toward the dock. He grabs a piling and hugs it hard, like a buoy in a falling sea. Frank breathes deeply until his panic—and the horrible vision it must have created— subsides, then duck-walks onto shore until the ice has turned to snow and the ground is assuredly beneath him. He slowly clomps up the slope. Beyond it will be the road, and the road will lead back to the house. He sniffs like a wounded animal—and smells smoke. Who but he and Jena could have a fire here? He limps toward the smoke smell, squints, and yes, there it is, dark against the night, the summer house, a thin plume of gray smoke unfurling from the chimney.

Frank goes around to the kitchen window and with a heavy grunt hauls himself through. He takes off his skates. With less strain on it, his ankle feels better. He lights the lanterns, gets a beer, and props his foot by the fire. He stares into the flames and lets their light and heat cauterize the awful vision from the ice. And then he's angry at Jena, furious. He fantasizes berating her for leaving him, or just leaving her and driving to a motel, *let her see how it feels.* And then he remembers the car, and how he's going nowhere.

And he's worried, too. *Could* something have happened to her? He hobbles to the front window and opens it. "Jena!" he yells. "Jena!" Neither beyond nor behind the gusting of the wind does he hear anything at all.

What can he do? He can't walk anywhere, there's no car, no phone to call the police . . .

All the children but one, he thinks, have come in from the darkening green. Suddenly he feels he understands the peculiar hauntingness and melancholy of that poem. The children, he realizes, are dead.

Twenty minutes, an hour later—he's lost track of time—Frank hears tramping in the yard. He goes to the kitchen window and helps her through.

"Hey," she says. Her face is flushed by excitement and exertion. "Wasn't it wonderful? My God—so *spooky!*"

"Where did you *go?*" He must try to talk measuredly, he knows, or his voice will change, into what he doesn't know, a cry of rage, a wail.

"All over!" she says. "It was just so spooky and great. Like flying through outer space." She pulls off her skates and sits by the fire. "God, I wish we had some hot chocolate. I'd *love* some hot chocolate."

"Why didn't you *answer* me out there? I kept calling for you."

"Did you?" She wraps her arms around her knees. "I couldn't hear you, I guess."

"I shouted!"

She shrugs. "The wind, probably."

"Why didn't you *wait* for me?"

She pokes the coals, which grumble and hiss. "I just thought you wanted to be alone."

"I was worried! I . . . I was frightened."

She looks at him. "Frightened?"

For a moment, all the fear and panic he felt out on the lake when he saw that horrible face, when he was sure the darkness above and below was coming to claim him, come rushing back, like wind through the cracks of the house, and he feels ashamed. How can he ever tell her?

"I was frightened for you," he says. It's at least partially the truth.

She grins. "You didn't have to worry about me. But it was awfully sweet of you." She pats the floor. "Come here. Sit by me."

Frank doesn't move. *"You* wanted to be alone, didn't you? That's really why you skated off, isn't it?"

Jena purses her lips, leans back on her elbows. Frank feels a clot in his throat. He swallows, but it won't go away. They both stare at the fire. In spite of its light, the room seems darker, smaller, as if they've let part of the night in.

"I guess I wanted to be alone, too," Frank says.

Jena crinkles her eyes. He doesn't know whether she believes what is, after all, a lie. And suddenly Frank understands that this is only one of many deceptions that will pass between them, that they are increasingly doomed to say things that they don't mean, that aren't true, until gradually the lies will become more important than anything, it is to the lies they will cleave, shivering in the dark, shorn of comfort, until their hearts freeze as fast and cold as the lake itself.

They are not the people they should have married. The thought is like a chill wind against his chest, and Frank wishes nothing more than to forget it.

"Did . . . did you worry at all about me?" he asks.

"Why? Should I have?"

"I fell. I think I sprained my ankle." He holds up his arm. "My wrist, too."

"Poor baby," she says. "Let's see." But he doesn't move. And neither, for that matter, does she.

Tombs

—Summer 1976

They *were in Greece,* on Crete, where Frank had been seven years before, and everything was different. Former dirt roads were paved, stores that once sold fish and olive oil now sold postcards, film, and T-shirts, buildings that would be hotels and American-style restaurants were going up everywhere. They'd been staying in Réthimnon, where Frank had lived that summer when he was trying to decide what he would be, and—ironically—whether or not he would marry Jena. He pointed out to her the window of his room above the newspaper, its front now plate glass, behind which a much bigger staff, each with a phone on his desk, was working. The *kafenion* he'd frequented mornings was much enlarged and now served "American breakfast"; the Odos Bar, however, was a shop selling ceramic sea gulls, sponges, and sea shells. Except for the fake Attic pottery, it could have been in Florida.

83

They'd climbed to the Fortezza where he'd spent afternoons sitting on the escarpments, waves foaming on the rocks
below. "I wrote postcards to you here," he told her, and she
nodded. "Those postcards," she said. Frank looked through a
crenellation at the sea, as if he might stare not only across space
but also back into time, and might turn to find his younger self
in torn shorts still sitting here scribbling, gazing dreamily into
an imagined future. Frank can see him, but he, sadly, cannot see
Frank. If he could only look over that young man's shoulder and
see what he's writing, Frank felt he might know something
about them both.

He'd looked forward to showing Jena around Crete: he
would be their guide, smooth their path, in a way that hadn't
been his—or theirs—for these last years of their marriage, and
definitely since her affair with Paul. Greece would allow something to happen, he hoped, some melting of the heart, a turning
in the axis of habit, that would allow them to be better, to grace
themselves, to find their way anew.

But it hadn't happened that way at all. Jena seemed
indifferent to his old haunts, although she loved Crete itself. She
was constantly taking pictures, and—to Frank's annoyance—
stopping to talk to shopkeepers, waiters, even children on the
streets. "Aren't the people wonderful?" she told him. "They're
what a place is all about."

To Frank, however, people seemed more short-tempered,
harried, surly than before. In the tavernas, waiters spoke English
now, however imperfectly, and were impatient when Frank tried
his Greek, efforts which they'd applauded years before. Fre-
quently they looked past him to Jena, who smiled and bantered
with them. The other night when Frank had asked to go into
the kitchen—the standard thing when he'd been there before,
since few tavernas had printed menus—the waiter shook his
head and pointed to a table. Irritated, Frank told Jena they were

leaving. "We don't have no hamburger, no hot dog," the waiter yelled after them, and Frank's face burned as he imagined everyone turning to stare. "What was that all about?" Jena asked. When Frank explained, she told him he'd acted childishly, and then they'd argued about that.

All the irritations that a happier couple might have shrugged off and laughed about and shared in the plucky way of fellow explorers only became more proof of their unhappiness. There was no escape: no matter where they went or what they saw, Greece was ready to remind them that they did not belong, they did not belong, they did not belong together.

On their fifth day in Crete they'd driven out from Réthimnon on the mountain road, the houses spread below like candy nougats in cubes of orange and blue and white. The sea was minty with summer. They were going to the Preveli Monastery, where they would have lunch and then drive through the Omphalos Gorge to the south coast and the Libyan Sea. They'd stopped in a village to consult their map when Jena grasped Frank's arm and pointed. Three children, a boy of about eight and two little girls of perhaps three and five, were standing with a black-haired goat by a fountain from which water poured into a stone trough. The little girls were holding the neck of the goat, which was festooned with red and blue ribbons and thick brass bells.

"I've just got to get a picture," Jena said.

As she approached, the little boy placed a protective arm around each sister's shoulders. They regarded her with wide eyes, neither suspicious nor friendly. She smiled and raised the camera. The smaller of the two girls squealed in embarrassment and delight, and turned her face, while her brother smiled grimly, as if he were accustomed to this picture taking, a ritual that must be tolerated.

"What's your name?" Jena asked the shy sister. The little

girl burrowed her head into her brother's shoulder. The goat tossed its head. "What's the Greek word for name, Frank?"

"I don't know." And then: *"Nomos."*

"Nomos?" The little girl shook her head.

"Jena, come on already," Frank called.

The boy spoke, his voice raspy, as if he were trying to make it more manful: "Maria." He solemnly pointed to the other little girl. "Eleni."

"And you?" Jena pointed.

"Nikos."

We'll never get to Preveli by lunch, Frank thought. He watched as Jena posed them separately, then together. The boy was puffing his chest a bit. *How confident he looks,* Frank thought. How aware he was, at such a young age, of his duties. Frank envied him.

"They were so cute," Jena said as they drove off again. "That little girl was so proud of her goat. I mean, you could've melted—"

"I just *thought* we were going to Preveli before lunch," Frank said. "Wasn't that the idea? Now we won't get there until one-thirty, and—"

"Oh, fuck Preveli! Who cares about another damn monastery?" Jena pulled her hair into a ponytail, then let it fall. "I mean, it's the people that make a country interesting, isn't it?"

"Friendly with everybody, aren't you?"

She looked at him. "Now just what does that mean?"

He gripped the wheel tighter. She kept looking at him.

"You're not going to leave it alone, are you?" she said.

"What?"

"Paul. This is really about Paul again, isn't it?"

"Do me a favor," Frank said. "Don't mention his name, okay? On my vacation, I don't need to hear about him. We've already talked enough about all that."

"I told you it's over, but you just won't let it rest, will you?"

"Jena, you're the one who brought him up. I wasn't thinking about him at all."

"Oh, I bet."

"Maybe it's not really so over for you, huh?"

"Jesus," she cried. "Frank, come on . . ."

"Maybe you'd rather *he* was here with you?"

"I don't know what's happened to you, Frank. My God, you—"

"I just don't want to hear his name, okay?"

Jena folded her arms and stared out the window. Olive trees whirred by in a swirl of silver and gray. A small truck carrying old tires passed them, honking like a frantic goose. She turned to face him, eyes defiant. "Paul, Paul, Paul, Paul, Paul . . ."

He worked his lips, concentrated on the road.

"Oh, what's the use?" She rubbed her forehead and again stared out the window.

Frank felt a small shameful triumph: he could still hurt her. Despite all that had happened between them, the slow accumulation of pain and grievance, its eruption into betrayal and hurt and anger this last year with her affair with Paul—and, Frank suspected, another man before him—in some way, she was still his.

"You sure picked the wrong person to go on a vacation with, didn't you?" Jena said. "Isn't that what you're thinking?"

"Let's just drop it, Jen. Let's try to have some fun."

"We don't have fun anymore."

The way she said this, so simply and final, made Frank's heart ache, so that only the shame remained. As so many times before, he wished and willed himself to have no more anger. Yet he kept stumbling upon it, dark and heavy and unyielding, when he least expected it, when he thought he'd put it away for good.

They passed an old woman leading a donkey with a crate on its haunches. They watched as she disappeared, Jena turning and staring over the back seat, he in the rear-view mirror. The rush of hot wind through the car windows blurred the chirring of the cicadas. Frank thought how they'd soon have to send postcards to their parents and lie about the wonderful time they were having. As they crested a curve, Jena touched his arm. "Wait! Slow down!"

He braked. "Now what?"

"A sign back there said something about Minoan tombs. It sounds spooky." Jena's eyes shone with a guileless expectation of danger and delight. *All right, forget Preveli,* Frank told himself. He would be amenable. They might yet salvage the day. He turned on the narrow road, and they went back.

There was a sign on this side, too, small and easy to miss. "Paleolithic Minoan Tombs Excavation," it said in English and Greek, with a small arrow pointing off the road. Frank and Jena turned onto a dirt trail, and within a hundred yards, in a declivity formed by two hills, they saw them: long rows of beehive mounds, like giant anthills, spread out over several acres. There were no signs of current excavation—no people or earth-moving equipment. They parked in front of a wooden barricade, the only car there.

"Not a big attraction," Frank said.

They got out. Without the breeze from driving, the heat was stifling. The cicadas sounded as loud as a waterfall. Frank shielded his eyes from the sun. "It looks closed," he said.

"Come on," Jena said. "If they wanted us out, there'd be a sign or something." She ducked under the barricade.

So easy, Frank thought. She just passed through, no hesitation, no fear. Was it possible that anything—to duck under a barricade, to change a life—could be done as easily? For the first time on the vacation, Frank felt a shiver of exhilaration, of possibility. He followed. Jena held out her hand, and he squeezed it. "Grave robbers," she said, grinning.

They gazed at the clay-colored hives. "So many," Jena said.

"I don't even know what we're looking at," Frank said.

She pulled the camera from her bag and snapped a picture. The cicadas, as if on signal, stopped. "God, that's spooky when they do that," she said. "Why do you suppose they do that?"

"I don't know. Getting their second wind, maybe."

"Maybe they're listening to us."

He laughed. And Jena did too.

"*Ola!*" From behind them, a cry. "Hey! *Ola!*" A man had emerged from an olive grove some thirty yards from the gate and was waving to them.

"Great," Frank said. "The guard."

The man was in his fifties, thick-waisted though not fat, his face broad and darkly tanned. His mustache and curly graying hair lent him the dignity of an old seaman, and indeed he walked with a lilt and a roll. He wore a blue cotton shirt, open to mid-chest, and jeans which were a little too tight. Give him a cutlass and a waistcoat, Frank thought, and he could have been an old-time pirate.

All right. They would apologize, smile all around, and leave. There was no blame, after all. They were tourists.

But the man was smiling. "Hey," he said. "*Guten Tag. Bonjour.*" The roll in his walk, the blinking of his eyes like an old turtle . . . *of course*, Frank thought. *He must have been napping down in the grove.* A soft job.

"Deutsch?" the man asked. *"Français?"*

Frank nodded. Jena shot him a glance.

"Bonjour, bonjour!" The man bowed slightly, a bit stiffly. Frank could smell a musky sourness, a mix of sweat and tobacco and alcohol.

"Not *français,*" Jena said. "We're American."

The man looked confused, then smiled broadly, as if the mistake had been his. "America, yes." He pointed up the hill, as if America were over there, beyond the strange mounds. "Many," the man said. He rocked gently in his thick-soled shoes. *"Mein Herr. Madame."* He started walking up the path through the tombs. "Come."

"Jesus," Frank whispered to Jena. "A goddam guide."

"Well, good. Maybe we'll find out what we're looking at."

"No we won't. He can't speak English, Jen."

"He seems to speak German."

"Well, *we* don't."

The man turned to see if they were following. "Many," he said again, sweeping his arm. "You see."

"Come on," Jena said, taking Frank's hand.

As they rounded a curve on the path, Frank could now see that there were even more tombs than he'd thought, row upon row of them. Many had stone steps uncovered by excavation which descended into the earth, below the domes.

"How many?" Frank asked. He held up his fingers, as if counting.

The man squatted, picked up a stone, and inscribed *180* in the dirt.

"One hundred eighty," Frank said to Jena.

"Many," she said to the guide. He nodded happily. She swept her arm around the site. "Who?" The man kept smiling, not seeming to understand. "What's the word for 'who,' Frank?"

"I can't remember." It bothered him—a simple word, and he couldn't recall it.

The guide rose and smacked the dirt from his hands. *"Mein Herr. Madame,"* he said officiously, ushering them up the path. "Please."

They followed. And Frank realized why the guide was so formal, almost unctuous: besides being a little tipsy, he was being overly careful, overacting an imagined role of "good guide."

"I don't think he's a real guide," Frank said to Jena. "He's just some guy who hangs around hoping to get a few drachmas from the tourists."

"Oh, who cares? He's showing us things at least."

"We could've seen all this by ourselves, Jen."

"He's just being nice, Frank."

"And he's drunk."

"He's a little tipsy. So what?"

The guide held up his hand at one of the tombs. Stone steps, heavily worn in the center, plunged steeply into the darkness twenty feet below. The guide ceremoniously gestured for them to descend. As Jena stepped forward, Frank saw him lightly grasp her elbow. *"Madame,"* he said. She smiled. He held her elbow solicitously as they went down into the tomb.

It was hard to believe such darkness and coolness were possible so close to the harsh sunlight and heat of the world above. Frank stood blinking on the earthen floor and felt, more than saw, that they were in a chamber whose roof rose some forty feet to the apex of the hive.

"Jena?" His voice sounded muffled in the enclosed space. He couldn't see her or their guide.

"Over here," she said. And then the guide flicked a cigaret lighter and he saw them only a few yards away, their faces
like masks floating in the dark. The guide lowered the lighter,
and in its light Frank could see two bathtub-shaped stone sarcophagi, the only objects in the chamber. The guide bent down,
put his lighter close to the side of one, and motioned for Frank
and Jena to come closer. They squatted beside him. A repeating
pattern of painted geometric animals snaked around the sarcophagus. *Horses?* Frank wondered. But horses weren't on Greece
in Paleolithic times, were they?

"My God, it's incredible these are just lying around
here," Jena said. "Anybody could come in and—"

The guide tapped the sarcophagus. *"Mann,"* he said. He
turned his lighter so that its flame illuminated the other one.
"Frau." He put the lighter on the sarcophagus, raised the index
fingers of both hands a foot apart, then brought them together,
so they were side by side, snuggled next to each other. In the
flickering half-light, he seemed almost leering.

"A husband and wife," Jena said.

Frank pointed to the sarcophagi. "Who?" And then he
remembered the word: *"Pios?"*

"Rich," the guide said. He scratched his palm with his
fingers to indicate great wealth. *"Capitalisti."* He picked up his
lighter and snapped it shut. They were plunged into such sudden
darkness that Frank started. He blinked. And then, in the weak
light trickling down from above, he saw them, the guide again
holding Jena's elbow while he ushered her up the steps. *He
doesn't have to do that,* Frank thought.

Above ground, the cicadas were thrumming lustily. A
flight of grackles flew from an olive tree, swirling silver and black
against the sky as they circled over the tombs and away. Frank
looked down the path; he could no longer see their car.

"Please," the guide said. He ushered them farther up the path. Jena fell back to rejoin Frank.

"Some guide," Frank said. "He doesn't know a goddam thing."

"It's sort of sweet in a way. Innocent."

"He's going to want a tip. Just for showing us what we could've seen ourselves."

"Who says we'd find all this by ourselves, Frank? Maybe some of the tombs are empty. I mean, he took us right to one that had those . . . those . . ."

"Sarcophagi."

The guide turned and smiled, as if knowing they were talking about him.

"And I don't like the way he's pawing you," Frank said. "Jesus, he takes your arm every chance he gets. It's not like you're an old woman or something."

"Oh, come on, Frank. He's just being courteous. It's kind of old-fashioned and sweet."

"It's *not* sweet. He's *pawing* you. And he's always trying to look down your dress. You know, getting ahead of you on the steps so he can look down—"

"Frank, come on."

"Why don't you wear a goddam *bra*, for God's sake?"

"Now stop it," she said sharply. "Just stop."

The guide held up his hand. He was standing at the entrance to a tomb shaded by two large plane trees. He went down a few steps, turned, and extended his hand. "Please." He reached for Jena's arm as she descended, but Frank, behind her, took it instead. The man stiffened and drew back. He followed them into the darkness of the tomb and flicked on his lighter.

This chamber's circumference was only half that of the first tomb, but there were at least a dozen sarcophagi, much smaller than those in the other tomb. The guide knelt beside one with its lid off and put the lighter on its edge. He looked at them and made a rocking motion with his arms. *"Kinder,"* he said.

Frank could hear Jena's soft intake of breath. She stepped forward, knelt down beside the guide, and peered into the sarcophagus as though the child might yet be inside. *"Kinder,"* the guide repeated.

She swept her arm. "All? Babies? *Kinder?"*

The guide nodded.

Jena rubbed her finger along the stone. She looked at Frank, her eyes glistening. "Such a small . . . such a small . . . baby."

"Jena," he said softly. He felt an impulse to kneel beside her, to touch her arm.

The guide pointed. "You? *Kinder?"* Frank shook his head. Jena rose, brushed her dress, and walked quickly toward the stairs. The guide followed, moving ahead, then turned to offer his hand. She shook her head fiercely. "No, I can walk fine. Please." She brushed past him up the steps.

In the sunlight once more, Frank caught up with her down the path toward their car.

"Jen, are you okay?"

She nodded. "Just fine." She stopped and wiped her eye with the palm of her hand. "Really." She sniffed hard and tried to cover it with a laugh. "It's all so stupid."

"You want to see any more?"

She shook her head.

He took her arm. "Then let's go, okay?"

She nodded.

When they reached the entrance, the guide, who had been following at a discreet distance, called to them. *"Herr. Madame."*

"No more," Frank said. "Madame's tired." He reached for his wallet.

"Please." The guide pointed to the grove of olive trees from which he'd first appeared.

Frank shook his head. "We don't want to see any more," he said. *"Nein."*

The man looked puzzled.

"Madame is tired," Frank said, pointing to Jena. He pulled a hundred-drachma note from his wallet and offered it to the guide, who stared at it. The man shook his head gravely. Again he pointed to the olive grove. *"Essen."* He made a shoveling motion to his mouth. "Okay? *Essen?"*

"He wants us to eat with him," Jena said.

"Jesus." Frank turned to the guide. "Thank you, but—

"Frank, let's do it."

He looked at her.

"I mean, he's taken his time to show us all this, he doesn't want money . . ."

"No, he just wants to look at your tits some more."

Jena's mouth tightened. She turned to the guide, who was watching them expectantly. "Okay," she said.

The man beamed. "Please." With a sweeping motion of his arm, he ushered them toward the grove.

Jena grasped Frank's hand tightly. "Just be nice," she warned.

"Madame, mein Herr." The guide seated them at a small wooden table, its blue paint heavily scaled. A breeze rustled through the olive trees, casting dark-sequined shadows over their faces, the table, the ground. Frank had the absurd feeling that they would be handed menus and a wine list. The man plopped a rucksack on the table, rummaged through it, and extracted an olive oil bottle half-full of a pale liquid. He held it up proudly.

He pulled out two glasses and set them down. As he poured them each a tumblerful, Frank saw him trying to peer down Jena's dress. *And with me right here,* he thought angrily.

"*Raki,*" the guide said.

I should do something, Frank thought. But what can you say to someone who doesn't speak your language? Become irate? Point to your wife's breasts and wag your finger? Grab her hand, despite her protestations, and leave?

Jena sniffed the drink. "What is it?"

"*Raki,*" Frank said. "Cretan moonshine."

The guide mimed drinking it, tossing his head back. "Is it safe?"

"All *raki*'s homemade," Frank said. "You take your chances."

The guide took a hefty swig from the bottle. He smacked his lips, wiped his mustache, and squatted beside them. "Good!" he said.

"Well, he's still alive." Jena sipped a little, and fanned her mouth. "Whew!"

The guide chuckled. "Good?"

"Good," Jena croaked.

The guide extracted a wedge of cheese and a thick slab of bread from his rucksack. He pulled a large jackknife from his pocket, cut three wedges from the cheese and three slices from the bread, and solemnly handed cheese and bread first to Jena, then to Frank. Was it his imagination, or did Jena bend over the table to afford the man an even better view of her breasts? The guide stuck the knife in the cheese, and took another swig of *raki.* "Good," he said.

Frank had no appetite. The breeze ruffled Jena's dress, her hair. The olive leaves crackled. The guide reached up and pulled an olive off a branch and bit into it. He chewed thoughtfully, scrunched his lips to indicate bitterness, and spat it out. Jena laughed. Frank drank his *raki,* and the guide poured him another tumblerful.

The man rose. Frank watched as he walked over to a patch of wild asphodels, picked a bunch, and came back. He handed them to Jena. *"Pour vous, Madame,"* he said, with mock shyness.

"Oh, my," Jena said, hand to breast, playing her part. "How lovely." She put them in her lap.

"Good?" The guide pointed to Frank's scarcely nibbled cheese. Frank nodded. The man looked pleased. Whether from heat or drink, Frank felt sweat on the back of his neck. His head already swirled from the *raki.* The cicadas' high-pitched whining seemed like a million small voices screaming at once.

Jena put her hands over her ears. "Very loud," she said to the guide. He stood, again reached up into the tree which shaded them, and snatched at a leaf. He uncupped his hand slightly to show them: a cicada, thick and black, like a stubby grasshopper. Frank was amazed. He'd never realized they were that close. You could just reach out and touch them.

The guide cupped his hands next to his ear. He listened, smiled, and held them to Jena's ear.

"Frank, you can hear him," she said with delight. "It's amazing! One single cicada."

The guide held his cupped hands for Frank to hear. They were rough and cracked, and smelled of cheese and tobacco. Frank heard nothing. He shook his head. The guide listened again and shrugged.

"Don't kill it!" Jena cried. They looked at her. Her eyes were wide, frightened. "Frank, tell him not to kill it." Frank looked helplessly at her, at the guide. He didn't know what to say, or how to say it. Whether he understood or not, the man opened his fist. The cicada fell to the ground. It wobbled for a moment, then flew away into the trees.

The guide poured the last of the *raki* into their glasses, then threw the bottle against a rock. It smashed, and Jena started. "Happy," the man said. He slapped his chest.

He's getting drunker, Frank thought.

With a flourish, the guide produced another bottle of *raki* from his rucksack. He grinned slyly, and pried out the cork with his knife. He started to refill Jena's glass.

"No more," she protested. "I'll be drunk." The guide turned down his lip, disappointed, and still tried to refill it.

"She doesn't want any more," Frank said sharply.

The guide looked at him, and for the first time Frank thought he saw something menacing, wolflike and raw, behind the man's clouded eyes. He poured the *raki* anyway.

"He doesn't take no for an answer," Jena giggled. She took a sip, let her head fall back, and closed her eyes. Frank could see fine beads of sweat on her upper lip. A vein in her neck throbbed. He watched it, fascinated. He glanced at the guide, and saw that he was looking at Jena, too.

"Jen, let's go," he said.

Jena fished the camera from her bag and pointed to the guide. "I've got to get a picture." He shook his head, made a small gesture of protest. "Yes, yes," Jena said, touching his arm. "With those tombs in the background. Go on." The guide reluctantly shambled over to where she was pointing. He put his hands on his hips and set his jaw in a pose of exaggerated dignity. "No, no," Jena laughed. "Act natural." The guide crossed his arms and mock-glowered. Jena snapped the picture. He started to walk back.

"Wait," Frank said. "Stay there." He turned to Jena. "Let's get a picture of the two of you together." She shrugged and handed him the camera. She walked over to the guide, who stood in a half-swagger.

Frank looked through the viewfinder. "A little closer." Jena moved next to the guide, who seemed to stiffen. "Raise your hat, Jena."

She tipped up her sun hat. "Like this?"

"Closer," Frank said. "Get closer. That's what you want, isn't it?"

Through the viewfinder he could see her eyes widen, her mouth open slightly as if to say something. She moved closer to the guide, their hips almost touching. "Like this?" she said in a clipped voice. "Or like this?" She looped her arm through the guide's arm. He looked startled, and glanced at Frank.

"Smile," Frank said. "Both of you." He snapped the picture. "I've got to do it again," he said. "Neither of you were smiling."

"Frank . . ."

He raised the camera.

"Hurry up, Frank," Jena snapped.

"Smile. I'm waiting for you both to smile."

Jena smiled tensely, while the guide looked confused.

"Okay," Frank said. "Got it."

Jena stalked back to the table. She snatched the camera, put it back in her purse, and sat down, hands folded, mouth tight.

"What?" Frank said, although he knew what.

She brushed her hair back, exhaled deeply.

"What?"

"Just tell me," she said tersely. "You think I want to fuck him, right?"

He reached for her arm. "Come on, let's go."

"No!" She yanked it away. "You tell me! You think I

want to slip down into one of those tombs and just do it, don't you?"

Frank looked at the guide, who, hearing them argue, stood apart.

"You think I want to fuck everybody, don't you?"

He pressed his knuckles on the table and leaned closer. "For Christ's sake, what should I think? You're running around with your boobs hanging out—"

"Goddam you," she hissed.

"—letting him paw you—"

"Oh, you're crude," she cried. "Filthy and crude and crazy."

"Come on. We're going!" He reached for her arm, and again she yanked it away. Frank glanced at the guide, who stood watching them, arms folded. Frank imagined that he understood everything, had understood from the beginning, if not by their words, then by their gestures, their intonations. He knew everything about them, and had only been waiting for them to reveal it to him and to themselves.

"Fuck you," Jena hissed. She rose and stalked out of the grove.

"Where are you going?" Frank cried. She turned up the path toward the tombs.

Behind him, the guide asked something in Greek. "I don't know what you're saying," Frank said.

"*Madame . . .*" The guide gestured.

"A fight," Frank said. "It'll be okay."

The guide started up the path after Jena.

"Come back here," Frank said thickly. But he didn't. Frank half-rose, then sat down. *Let her go,* he thought angrily. *Let them both go.* He drank the rest of his *raki.* It burned his throat. He drank what was left in Jena's glass. The cicadas' chirring seemed to be coming from inside his head. He threw the glass into the tree, but they weren't silenced at all, and it clinked dully on the ground. Frank walked back to their car. The interior was an oven. He sat with the door open, half-in, half-out.

I'm not going to go after her, he told himself.

But after some minutes—five, ten, he didn't know— when Jena hadn't come back, Frank went back under the gate and up the path. The cicadas had stopped. Except for the crinkle of the olive leaves, everything was silent.

"Jena?" he called.

What if it were true? What if out of spite, she had . . .

Horrifyingly, sickeningly, he imagined Jena and the guide urgently making love in one of the tombs. He walked faster. "Jena!" he cried. The path forked. Which way had she gone? There were so many tombs . . .

And if he found them, what would he do? Scream in unknown languages? Turn back, get in the car, drive away? Fight? The guide was thick-muscled, he had that knife . . .

This is crazy, Frank told himself. He sat on the steps of a half-excavated tomb, the dirt piled high to the side. His mouth tasted dry and leaden. He breathed deeply to calm himself. He looked around. If only she appeared right now, he might yet take her hand and say he was sorry, it was all foolishness, all he really wanted was for her to just . . . come back. *But no, she won't come,* Frank thought. She was too stubborn for that. She was somewhere with *him,* in one of the tombs . . .

"All right," Frank said aloud. All right, he would no longer expect her to come back, if this is what she wanted, all right. He walked back toward the entrance. He would wait in the car and she could come whenever she damn well would. They'd go back to Réthimnon and Athens and home. They would end this horrible vacation, they would end their marriage, they would end everything.

When Frank arrived back at the gate, he saw the guide

standing close to one of the olive trees in the grove where they'd eaten lunch. He was humming and urinating. Jena was nowhere in sight. The guide zipped up his pants and went to the table. He picked up his knife and wiped it on his pants.

"Hey," Frank cried. The man squinted, as if he'd forgotten who Frank was. His face seemed redder, puffed from sun and drink. He closed the knife and put it in his pocket.

"Where's my wife?" Frank asked.

The guide picked up the glasses and stuffed them in the rucksack.

"Madame—" Frank said. *"Pou ine?"*

"She go." The man waved toward the car, the road. He pulled tight the thongs on his rucksack and shouldered it. He was going too.

"No, wait. *Pou ine?" She couldn't have left without the car,* Frank thought.

The man grunted, and walked past him.

"She's still here, isn't she?" Frank cried. He pointed to the ground. "Here?"

The man waved his fingers impatiently. "She go, *go.*"

"But the car's still here." Frank pointed. "Car. *Car.*"

The guide shrugged and mimed hitchhiking.

"She wouldn't do that," Frank said. "She—"

And suddenly Frank saw it all, saw the man drunkenly grabbing Jena, clawing at her dress, and Jena resisting, and he in a drunken rage hitting her, or worse . . . Like a scene illuminated in a shudder of lightning, Frank saw Jena dead, broken or strangled or bloodied from a knife wound, lying—where? Behind those olive trees? In one of the tombs? She could be anywhere, if not dead, then dying—he had to make the man, already at the gate, tell him . . .

"Wait!" he cried. The man turned and looked at him.

And what would Frank say now? He had no language for his fear,
no words for what he needed to know. *I should grab him,* he
thought, *shake him, make him tell me*—even as he realized he
could never, never do it.

The guide smiled thinly, as if he knew all this too. He
turned, ducked under the gate, and was gone down the path,
rucksack slapping against his back.

Frank ran among the tombs, shouting Jena's name, his
panic mounting. He stumbled down the steps into one of the
mounds, but could see nothing, it was too dark—*she could be
anywhere*—there were too many, too many . . .

"Jena!" He was almost crying. He ran back to the car. He
would drive for help. There would be police somewhere—yes,
back in Réthimnon—he would get them, they would come and
search for her. He saw all that was going to happen: saw them
finding her bloodied body, saw the funeral, saw his life without
her in all its sorrow, its strange and heady mix of grief and
freedom, his future filling his lungs like bitter smoke, so that he
was made dizzy and reeling.

I've got a past now, he thought as he drove up the trail
to the main road. He blinked with shame as he realized he also,
in the most horrible way imaginable, had a future.

"Jena," he murmured. "Oh God, Jena."

A quarter-mile down the road, he saw her. She was walking along the edge, arms swinging purposefully. He stopped, and
opened the door. She looked at him warily, then got in. She sat
with her arms folded, chin down. Frank felt his fear and grief
and, yes, exhilaration, drain from him like water over cobble-
stones, like shadows creeping back from the course of noon.

She was mulling something. He expected silence, he expected cries, he expected anger and castigation. And yet when
Jena finally spoke, she said something he never expected.

"Thanks for picking me up." She said it with neither anger nor irony.

He reached over and took her hand, and she let him. He looked not at her, but at the road, blinking hard, harder, as if it were very bright and he must concentrate.

"I saw one of those wild goats on the hill right before you came," Jena said after a while. "Those—what do you call them?"

He thought. *"Agrimi."*

"Agrimi . . ." She turned it over on her tongue. "You know the word for everything, don't you?"

They drove back to where they'd come from, and the silence in the car was like the silence of a tomb.

Feral Cats

—*October 1977*

When *I pull into* the drive of the summer house, heat lightning is making the afternoon sky flare with a hard, steelish glow. My mother's car is parked near the back porch. She's there, just as my father said she'd be. I've come all the way from Michigan to see her, yet now I'm reluctant to get out of my car. I sit looking at the lightning over the lake. When I was little, my mother used to tell me that heat lightning was God winking and blinking at us. I watch it now, content just to feel the mugginess of the air, the expectancy of the afternoon.

My father called two nights ago to tell me that my mother had run off to the summer house. That's how he put it: "run off."

"She left a note," he told me. "She says she wants to be by herself for a while and I shouldn't come after her. She's like some damn elephant wandering off . . ." He cleared his throat. "I wish you'd go, Frank. She shouldn't be there in her condition. Tell her to get back home."

"Dad, I'm three hundred miles away." Soon after Jena and I separated for good, I'd left California to take a new job in Michigan—California was a huge state, but somehow too small now. "Besides," I told my father, "what good would it do for me to go there?"

"It'll be different with you, Frank. She sees me all the time. I . . . I fuss over her too much." He cleared his throat again, a little too roughly, and I realized how upset he was. "It's me she's tired of. But she's always happy to see you." And then he said something which I knew was hard and which was the measure of his distress: "Please. Please go." Because of that, and because I was worried too, I went. I took a morning flight to Erie, rented a car, and got up here by mid-afternoon.

Nobody has come out yet. Maybe she's resting. Or gone for a walk. I open the car door and step out. And just as I do, a large mottled dog, an ugly godforsaken mixed breed, darts from behind the house, growling and snarling. I jump back in the car. I roll the window down halfway. "Get!" I yell. "Get out of here!" Unafraid, the dog comes right up to the door, his lips curled back to show his fangs.

"Hush up! Get away, damn you!" My mother appears on the porch. She's holding a baseball bat which looks much too heavy for her. "Stay back, Mom," I yell, but she slowly comes down the steps, hunched a bit, still favoring the side of her operation. "Mom! Don't—" The dog turns and looks at her, then, amazingly, trots off around the house and into the woods.

I get out of the car.

"So you came," my mother says, walking toward me. "I

see it all. Your father called and asked you to come get me and you came. Well. All right." She holds her arms out stiffly, and we embrace. I kiss her lightly on the cheek. Her skin feels dry and papery. She seems lighter, frailer than when I saw her last, only a month ago, back in Tyler; when I squeeze her arm, I can feel the bone. She's wearing jeans and one of my father's plaid work shirts, much too large for her. Her head is covered with a red kerchief. A few wispy strands of what hair she has left poke through the edges.

We walk up to the house. "Where the hell did that dog come from?" I ask. Behind us, there's a distant growl of thunder.

"I don't know. He was just hanging around when I got here. Probably left by one of the summer people. It's just amazing what they abandon."

"God, he's an ugly one."

"Isn't he, though?" She stops and looks at the spot where the dog disappeared into the woods. "He hangs around because of the cats."

"Cats?"

She nods. "We've got a whole colony of feral cats living under the porch. Ones that've been abandoned over the years. We've had them—oh, must be three or four years now."

"Jesus." I glance at the porch. "How many?"

"It's funny, there never seem to be more than ten or so. The winter probably does them in something fierce. And then there's other animals—like that damn dog. As long as they stay under the porch, they're okay, he can't squeeze in there. But he's always hanging around waiting." She sighs. "There was a cute little orange-and-black tabby I'd almost made friends with. I almost got her to come and take food from my hand. But I haven't seen her since Tuesday. I'm afraid he got her."

"Well, *you* sure seem to scare him," I say.

She shakes her head. "I don't think I really scare him at all. He never goes too far off."

She's walking stiffly, more noticeable when we go up the porch steps. "Do you hurt, Mom?" I ask.

She opens the screen door. "Hurt? No. Thanks for asking, honey, but no."

We go inside. It's much cooler in the house. The last time I was here was in winter, with Jena, when we'd broken in like mischievous kids. *I never did repair that broken window latch,* I think. I look around at the knotty-pine furniture, the faded slipcovers, the print of Lake Leman over the fireplace. I smell the familiar odor of damp wood and shellac and mildew. It smells like childhood, like all the summers I've ever had. It smells as if I never should forget it.

"You know, that's my old baseball bat," I say.

My mother looks at it, as if just now recognizing what it is. "I just found it in here. I've been using it to prop open a window. It's been so hot and I like getting the breeze." Her voice trails away. "Did you play baseball up here?"

"Not much. There weren't a lot of other kids around."

"I don't remember." She seems puzzled, as if searching for a memory of me, summer, baseball. She tries to raise the window to put the bat back in. I see she's having difficulty, so I go over to help.

"I can do it," she snaps.

I push it up anyway, shove the bat inside. She's panting a bit. *Just from trying to raise the window,* I think.

"I could've done it," she says. She looks around, as if there's something else to do. "Do you want a soda? I've got some Coke—no, Diet Pepsi. Or I could make iced tea."

"Pepsi's fine," I say. "You don't have to make me anything." I follow her into the kitchen. She gets the sodas from the fridge, cracks some ice, and pours. I go over to the sink and look at the window latch Jena broke. It's been fixed, of course—my father, I'm sure. My mother hands me a glass, and we go back to the front room and sit in facing chairs by the window. Thunder rumbles. To be autumn and to be so hot, I think. As if summer, like a reluctant guest, were refusing to pack up and go.

"Well, you look good," she says.

"So do you," I lie. When I talk with her and my father on the phone, she always says she's fine, and even though I don't really believe it, know she's being stoic and uncomplaining, still I'm startled to see how much frailer she's become in just a month. She seems to be conserving herself in little ways, her movements smaller, more considered. Her step is hesitant, as if she had to think more about where to go and how to get there.

She carefully places her glass on the end table. "All right. What did your father tell you?"

"He's worried about you, Mom. He—"

"He doesn't think I can survive without him." She laughs sharply. "He tells me I'm doing fine, but then he goes into fits if I just . . . go off for a while."

"Well, he worries, Mom." I pause. "I do too."

"Don't. I'm doing fine. I just wanted to get off by myself a bit, that's all." She rubs her thigh. "Can't somebody have a little rest after what I've been through?"

A car drives by, and a bottle smashes on a rock.

"I didn't really get a summer this year," she says. "So I'm taking one now."

We sip our drinks and look out the window, across the lake. In just the past twenty minutes, its color has darkened from azure to ultramarine. A breeze riffles its surface, vanishing before it reaches our shore.

"You've got some gray," she says. "I just noticed."

"A little bit," I say self-consciously.

"Imagine—I lived to see a child of mine getting gray." She chuckles. "Do you want chicken for dinner? I've got a chicken. And some corn on the cob."

"Anything. Don't fuss."

"I don't really eat much myself, but I couldn't resist that corn down at the road stand. I got those peonies"—she points to a vase of red and blue flowers on the mantel—"there too."

We talk a little about people back in Tyler, about my apartment, about Jena. "She wanted me to give you her love," I say, even though Jena hadn't said that. Beyond saying how terrible she felt about my mother's illness, she hasn't said much at all. "I've got a book I want to send her," she told me once on the phone. "About positive stress therapy." I told her maybe my mother would like that.

"Did Jena ever send you a book?" I ask.

"A book?"

"She said she might."

"No, I haven't heard from her at all." I can see the hurt in her eyes, dim and liquid and ghostly, and I wish I hadn't said anything. "She's probably busy."

The breeze is stronger now. The curtains swell and pop, swell and pop. My mother takes a deep breath and closes her eyes. "Well, you could sure fool me. It sure smells like summer." She looks at me. "It's wonderful to see you, honey. You stay tonight. You stay and we'll have a nice dinner. I wouldn't want you to drive in a storm anyway. But tomorrow, you go back. Call Dad, tell him not to worry. Tell him I'm . . . getting stronger here. Tell him anything you want. All right?"

She seems to straighten a bit as she talks, color rising in her cheeks, and I imagine maybe she *will* be fine, just like she says, will get stronger, despite everything. It's almost like being a child again, scared by branches scraping against the window or shadows passing across the walls, and having her come and say something to comfort me, which is always the same thing: *There's nothing to be afraid of, there are no ghosts, everything will be all right.*

"I'm going out and do a little yard work," she tells me. "Before it rains. Those leaves need raking."

"Mom, why? Who cares what the yard looks like? Why tire yourself out?"

She shrugs.

"Every fall you've been gone by this time and the leaves piled up and did just fine without anybody raking them."

"Well, I'm here now," she says. "I might as well do it."

I rise. "I'll do it then. You just—"

She's shaking her head. "Please. Humor me."

"I don't want you—"

"You're just like your father," she scolds. I feel myself flush. "Two of a kind."

"I'm not like him," I say.

She rises and buttons the sleeves of her shirt. "Honey, if you want to help, get the chicken out of the freezer. Husk the corn." She puts on a floppy sun hat over her kerchief, and walks out onto the porch and down the steps.

Who can argue with her? I think. I go to the kitchen and take the chicken out of the freezer, the corn out of the vegetable bin. Dirty dishes are piled in the sink. The perk coffee pot—my mother's never made it any other way—is full of souring grounds. I pour them into the grocery bag she's using for garbage. I wipe off the counters. I run water for the dishes, squeeze in soap. I look out the window and see my mother slowly scratching at the leaves in the side yard. I turn off the water and watch. She seems to be having trouble getting one leaf onto the pile she's making. She stabs at it with the prongs of the rake and, after a few unsuccessful stabs, finally spears it. But now it won't come off, no matter how hard she shakes. She contemplates it. Then she bends over, ever so slowly, as if her whole insides hurt or would jar loose if she moved too quickly. Her hat falls off. She takes the leaf off the prong and gently drops it on the pile, then bends deeper to pick up the hat. She carefully places it on her head.

Something has attracted her attention now—her brow furrows and she puckers her lips, as if she's going to whistle, then tightens them, concentrating. I lean over the sink to see what she's looking at. She dips at the knee, as if she's going to genuflect. She puts the rake down and makes a chucking sound.

And then I see it, moving cautiously through the leaves: a black-and-orange cat. It is thin, its ribs ragged, its steps distrustful. With each one, it seems to sniff the air. My mother stops clucking, and holds out her hand, as if to reassure it. The cat stops, and they are frozen in tableau. *It won't come,* I think, *it will run off.* But then it takes a long, arched step, as if crossing some divide. My mother makes soft sounds, as if the cat were a child she was encouraging to take its first steps, and I wonder, *Did she talk to me that way when I took mine?* The cat's whiskers twitch, it is only a few feet from her. My mother extends her hand, palm down, turning it slowly, as if to show the cat that nothing is concealed, and then, hardly touching it at first, she pats it—once, then again.

My eyes mist. I turn on the water, just to do something, and when I look back, the cat is dashing off, my mother kneeling, one hand still extended, puzzled and defeated. She stands up, and then, only now remembering, slowly stoops again to pick up the rake.

How did we ever come here, I wonder, *to be doing what*

we are? I'm washing dishes and my mother's raking leaves and trying to pet a wild cat. How have our lives led to this? How could any of us have foreseen this moment? How could we ever have known it would be important?

The porch door creaks and slams as she comes back in. I wash the dishes, dry them, and empty the water in the sink. It sucks down with a strained gurgle. The thunder is closer, more insistent. When I go into the front room, the sky over the lake is dark, like an overripe plum. My mother is sitting in the armchair, the lamp on. Her head rests in her hand, one finger extended along the line of her jaw to her temple, right below the pulse beating there. Her eyes are closed. I sit in the chair across from her. She opens her eyes, smiles sheepishly. "I must have dozed," she says.

"I saw you from the window. With the cat."

She smiles. "She let me touch her. For the first time."

"You should be careful. Those cats may have rabies or something." I don't know why I say that—I never even thought about it until this moment.

"She only let me touch her once," my mother says. "Then she just dashed off. I don't know what I did." She looks at me, as if I can tell her. "She's the only one of them that's even let me get close."

We hear a rustling and a furious bounding in the leaves. Something fast and heavy. "The dog," she whispers.

"I'll go look."

I open the screen door and walk out onto the porch. The shadows in the woods are already steep and black. I'm on the second step when I hear it again—a dart and a dash through the brush. I crane my neck. Something is out there, but I can't see it. I go back in.

"It's that dog, isn't it?" my mother asks.

"I don't know, Mom. It could have been anything."

"Damn him!" She stands up—almost too quickly, it seems, because she grasps the chair arm a moment for support. I think she's about to go out there into the woods after him, but then she says, "I'll make something for you to eat, honey. I'm not too hungry myself." She grins. "This whole business has helped my figure, at least."

THE CHICKEN HASN'T defrosted, and I haven't husked the corn, so my mother makes a tuna salad instead. After preparing it, she opens another can of tuna into a bowl. "For the cats," she explains. "Maybe they'll come out to eat and we'll see them." She puts it outside on the steps, then comes back in to sit and peck at her own food. In the background, the radio's tuned to a soft-music station from Buffalo. At last she gives up pretending to eat and lays her fork across the edge of the plate, exactly parallel to her knife. She sips her glass of water, delicately licks her lips as if to partake of every bit of moisture.

"You know," she says, "I can't hear music anymore. It just escapes me. I listen hard, I hear each individual note, but the *whole* thing escapes me somehow." She folds her hands on the table. "Maybe that's what dying's like. You start to pay less attention. You can't grasp the whole thing."

"Mom, I wish you wouldn't talk like that. You don't know you're dying."

She laughs sharply. "I wouldn't place any bets, honey."

"Who says that? Does the doctor say that?"

She shakes her head. "Oh, you're right. This is silly. Let's not talk about this." She's silent, and I think she's trying to listen to the music, but then she says, "Do you remember that friend of yours? The barber?"

"Tommy Kozella?"

She nods. "He died a few months ago."

"My God. How?"

"Some kidney thing, I think. Left two little boys."

I hadn't seen Tommy in years. I thought of the break-ins of our adolescence, and how out of all of us, crazy young kids that we were, he might have been the most pure, the fairest. He was satisfied with the least, and the least made him happy. He'd probably been a good father, I thought.

We sat for a while in silence.

"Do you know what happened to Ira Dunn?" I asked.

"Ira Dunn? Ricky Dunn's cousin?"

I nodded. "I heard a rumor he went to Vietnam."

She shook her head. "Ricky left Tyler a long time ago. Ira I never knew. I didn't know he was a friend of yours."

"He wasn't exactly."

"You never had him over to the house."

I look at her. "No."

Again, we're silent.

"Mom," I say at last, "why'd you come up here?"

"I told you—to be by myself a bit."

"Is there . . . something wrong between you and Dad?"

"No. Oh no. He's very sweet, your father. He's . . . the best. It's been a great strain for him"—she waves her hand—"all this. Me." She stops and folds her hands again.

"Mom, what's wrong?"

"What's wrong?" Her gaze is so fierce I'm frightened. "Do I really have to tell you what's wrong?"

And then the fire fades from her eyes, just drifts away, only smoke left now, and its sting. Her eyes are burned out, almost hollowed. I take our plates over to the sink and scrape her uneaten salad into the bag. I come back and sit down, then get up again. I've got to get out, walk around a bit. Besides, I tell myself, I should call my father and let him know I'm here, that my mother's okay.

"Where are you going?" she asks.

"Down to Duchene's. To get some beer."

"It's not Duchene's anymore, you know. It's a Mini-Mart now."

"What happened to Duchene?" Before I even finish saying it, I know. She doesn't even have to answer. "I'm going to call Dad too," I say quickly.

"Oh you are, are you?"

"Mom, he's worried. He wants to know how you are."

She opens her mouth, takes in a breath as if she's going to argue, but says, "All right."

"Can I tell him when you're coming back?"

"I told you—just tell him not to worry. Tell him"—she spreads her hands—"to be of good cheer."

"Frank." I'm at the door when she calls. I turn. She raises her hands to her head and slowly unwinds her kerchief. For the first time since the operation and therapy I see her without kerchief, without wig. What is left of her hair is scraggly and patchy, like a baby's. Purplish marks dot her scalp. She looks at me, at once defiant and shy. I don't know what to say, then realize she doesn't want me to say anything, just wants me to see.

"I'll do the dishes when I get back," I tell her. I walk out and down the porch steps and for a moment I feel dizzy, as if I'm not here at all but on the edge of a deep, far cliff, it's night, I don't know where I'm going, and I think with shame, *That had to be the stupidest thing I've ever said.*

WHEN I GET BACK from the Mini-Mart, my mother's lying on the sofa, eyes closed, hand across her brow, kerchief back in place. She seems asleep. I walk softly into the kitchen, open a beer, put the rest of the six-pack into the refrigerator. I see that she's already washed the dishes. I go back into the front room. The radio's still playing. I turn it off.

"Don't," she says, not opening her eyes. "I was trying to listen."

I turn it back on.

"Are you tired, Mom? Do you want to go to bed?"

"I'm just resting my bones."

"You don't . . . hurt, or anything?"

She shakes her head. She points to the lamp beside the sofa. "Will you just turn that shade a bit, honey? It's shining right in my eyes."

I do that, then sit down. I gaze out the window and across the lake. The heat lightning flashes like semaphore.

"Lord, I wish it would just *do* it," she says. "Either rain or pass over. It just seems to get muggier and muggier and not *do* anything." She sighs. "Did you see if the cats ate any of the fish?"

"It's all still there."

"Maybe they'll come out later. They're so *shy.*" She turns her head to look at me. "Well, what'd he say? Your father?"

"He wants you to come back. He says if you don't come back soon, he doesn't care what you say, he's going to come up. He said it's only because I'm here right now that he hasn't done it already." She smiles. "He says he should spank you."

"Did he say all that?" She chuckles. "Well, well."

She lies there, and I sit, in silence. Or not quite silence, because a strong breeze is gusting through the trees now, the leaves rustling like old promises. Thunder curls overhead. Behind it all, the radio, the melodies of old songs.

"So tell me," she says. "How is Jena?"

"Okay, I guess. We don't really talk much anymore."

"She's still in the house?"

I nod. "We're trying to sell it."

"I never saw your house," she says, almost wistfully. "I don't know why we never came to California." She sighs. "Two stay-at-homes, your father and me." She turns her head. "And your job? How's it?"

"I told you, Mom. Like the other one. Just writing technical manuals. Nothing special."

"Why don't you do something you really *like*, honey?"

I press the tips of my fingers together, hard. "I'm doing okay."

"You always talk about your work as if . . . it's a penance, or something."

"I do?"

Her eyes search mine, and I grin—foolishly, I think.

"I just would like to see you more *settled,*" she says.

"Mom, stop. Okay?"

We're silent again.

"You know, Richard Halliburton came to my school once," she says. "When I was in fifth grade." My mother rubs her temples. "Do you know who he was?"

"An explorer, right? Kind of like Lowell Thomas?"

She gives a sharp little laugh. "*Better* than Lowell Thomas! Lowell Thomas was a reporter. Halliburton was an *explorer.* He climbed the Pyramids. He was bit by a fer-de-lance in . . . India, I think. He rafted down the Nile. Oh, he was something! And so tall and blond and handsome. I had a book he wrote about his travels. I read it and reread it, and I wouldn't lend it out to anybody, not even my best friend, Ruth Ann Gilliam.

"He went around the country giving lectures. And one

day he came to our school! I couldn't believe it—Richard Halliburton in little poky Oshtohola. It was like the President coming—no, it was better than that. It was like God coming. I was
so excited! It was winter, and I was so anxious I'd get a cold or
something and miss him that I went straight home every day
after school for a whole week and stayed inside."

"So how was he?"

"Oh my. He showed slides in the auditorium. Black-and-
white. He had some big clumsy projector. It smelled like something burning." Her voice has become softer—not quieter,
exactly, just more dreamy. "He had an assistant who ran it, some
little darkish-type fellow who looked Indian, and I wondered
whether he was a *slave* or something that Halliburton had freed
from his evil master." She laughs, and I do too.

"It's funny—I don't remember what he talked about at
all. I don't think I remembered even ten minutes later. I was just
so excited to *see* him. He didn't look as tall as the picture in my
book, but then, I was sitting way back." She chuckles. "I don't
even remember the slides. Oh, one—him on a big camel,
with a turban. No, not a turban exactly, one of those sheik-type
things . . ."

"Burnoose?"

"I guess. He had one of those wrapped around him.
That's all I remember from that whole day. I was eleven years
old."

Thunder rolls over the house, and now the first flash of
hard lightning. *We're really going to get it,* I think. A gust of
sharp wind comes through the window, lifting the curtains like
shy skirts. I can smell the rain, thick and yeasty. It smells like
the East, hay and mushrooms and wild, wet clover.

"He was probably just a big fake anyway," she murmurs.
"No, he probably wasn't."

"Maybe I'd better close the windows, Mom."

She looks at me. "I'm trying to tell you that I'm not sure I've lived the right life."

We sit there, rain pattering on the roof, *thocketa, thocketa.*

"Does that include me, Mom?" The words stick like tiny bones in my throat.

She's still looking at me, and her smile is tired.

"Are you that disappointed with me?"

"Listen." She raises a finger. " 'Begin the Beguine.' I love this song." She pushes herself to a sitting position. "Let's dance."

"Mom—"

"Come on." She stands up and holds out her hand. "Your father never dances with me."

"Mom, no—"

"Don't you dance?"

"Not really."

"You didn't dance with Jena?"

"Sometimes," I say impatiently.

"This song always makes me think of moonlight. Pools and pools of moonlight." She holds out her hand, beckoning. "Oh come on."

I sigh. I get up and take her hand, stiffly put my arm around her waist. We shuffle a bit, at arm's length. I wish the song would end, but it drones on.

" . . . *a night of tropical splendor* . . . " my mother sings softly, over the rain. She moves a bit closer in my arms. I can feel her papery skin, smell something weary and stale. To my shame, I want to push her away, and maybe she senses that, because suddenly she stops. "Lord, I *am* tired." She says it simply, a fact, nothing more. She goes back to the sofa and lies down. "You know, I always wished I could play the piano. It would've been nice to have had more music in our house. I could've played this." She chuckles. "*I* should've taken lessons, not you."

"I'm going to close the windows," I say. I go to the front windows, take the baseball bat out of one, and push it down. It falls easily. The next, however, is swollen hard, tight, and won't budge.

"When I was a little girl," she says, "I'd always try to figure out which way the rain was coming from. Then I wouldn't have to go close every window in the house, just the ones where the rain might come in. I was always trying to figure out ways out of housework. I was a lazy little girl. Lazy, lazy, lazy." She lets her arm fall from the sofa. "Look at me now."

I push the window hard, with a savage grunt, and it slams shut, the pane rattling.

"Easy, honey," she says.

Outside, a cat yowls, a horrible, piercing cry. My mother sits up. "The dog!" Her eyes are wide and frightened. "The dog—he got her!"

"Easy, Mom."

"No, no—I heard!" She goes out onto the porch.

"Mom," I shout, "it's just a cat mating or—" The porch door slams. I run out; she's already down the steps. "My God, Mom, get out of the rain!" She picks up the bowl; half the tuna is gone.

"She was *eating*," she says. She holds the bowl for me to see. "She was eating, and he got her."

"Mom, get *inside!*" I go down the steps and tug at her arm. Reluctantly, she lets me lead her back in. She sits down on the sofa. "You've got to dry off," I tell her, and she nods. I take the bowl from her hands and go into the kitchen. As I'm rinsing

it, she comes in, still soaked, a determined, almost glazed look
in her eyes. She opens the refrigerator, takes out the chicken,
and puts it on the counter, then begins opening cabinets, shuffling through boxes and glasses and jars. She pulls out a yellow-
and-red box. Rat poison.

"Mom?"

She walks past me as if I'm not even there, and I think,
my God, she's going back out there again, into the rain, and I
follow her and grab her arm just as she's about to descend the
steps. She yanks. "Let me go!" she cries, but I hold her.

"What are you *doing?*" I demand.

" . . . kill him . . ." she says thickly.

"Who?"

"The dog, the *dog!*" In the light spilling from the front
room, I can see tears in her eyes. "I'm going to poison him!"

"Mom, that's crazy!" She pulls again, hard, but I hold
her. "You don't know what happened. You don't—"

"He's out there," she says. Her eyes are feverish. "I
know!"

"Well, you *can't* poison him." I grip her arms tightly, and
suddenly I'm afraid I might start shaking her, like a broom, a
rattle. I let go. She stands there, saying nothing, rain spattering
against the screen. She's looking at me with what I imagine to
be hate. And the words are blurted out before I even realize I'm
saying them. "Why can't you just go quietly! Why are you
making it so hard—"

My mother blinks. Her hand flies to her throat as if
something has caught there, and I'm sorry, just so sorry I said
this. I take the chicken and the rat poison from her hands and
go back inside. I toss the chicken in the garbage and put the
poison back in the cupboard. I think again, and take it back out.
I could pour it down the sink, but instead I squat and put the

poison behind the refrigerator. *Hiding things from my mother,* I think.

I go into the front room to say I'm sorry, but she's not there. I listen. She's already gone upstairs. Upstairs I can hear her making my bed, for me to sleep in.

I go out onto the porch and stare through the screen into the driving rain, as if by concentrating, just by thinking *hard* about it, I could see through the dark to what is, after all, only more rain, and the lake beyond, and the forest beyond that, darkness here and darkness there. Nothing to see at all. And I wonder: What do blind men feel standing on a porch like this, by a lake, in the rain? Do they smell the wet air and dank leaves, feel the planking beneath them tremble in thunder, sense the uncertainness of water, the evanescence of air?

I go upstairs, but my mother is in the bathroom now. In my room, lightning dances along the wall. I pick up the ship in a bottle that I'd made when I was a boy and finger the cold, rough glass. I put it down. I open all my old, empty drawers. The few clothes I brought with me are hardly worth putting in there. I listen, then go into my mother's room. Her suitcase is open on the floor. It's heavily riffled; evidently she's been taking clothes out only as she needs them. On the end table is a book, her place marked by a slip of note paper. *The Thai: The Enchanted People,* I read. Checked out from the Tyler Public Library. I open the book and look at the slip of paper. It's a list she's made:

> 7 am—Medicine, stretch muscles
> till 11—Lawn, or walk a bit
> 11—Medicine? Or skip if feeling good
> 1 pm—Rest, if necessary
> 3—Read
> 5—Grieve

There's more, but I can't read any further. I put the list back in the book, the book on the table, and sit down on the edge of the bed. I don't know what I'm feeling, only that it has no weight, no dimension, other than overwhelming. I put my arms around my shoulders and rock, back and forth, like an old woman, like a child. I feel something raw and wet and shameful rising in my throat, and I want to tell her that I was the one who broke into our house in Tyler all those years ago, that I was the one who broke into this house years later, and who left without repairing the window latch. Me, me, it had always been me.

I shouldn't be here, I think, *in my mother's room.* I tiptoe back to mine. Soon the bathroom door opens, the light is switched off. I feel I'm a little boy again, waiting for her to come to my room when I've been bad. She will come, and I will—what? Apologize? But already I know the moment has passed, and I can't. *But why not?* I wonder. And the answer comes: Because I wouldn't know what to apologize for, if not, somehow, for everything.

But she goes to her room. Once, twice, I hear her trying to close the humidity-swollen door. I hear her bed creak as she lies down. And then, except for the soft shirring of the rain against the roof, the house is quiet.

Everything, I think, *ends badly.*

When I wake in the night, the rain is falling in torrents. Someone is standing at the foot of my bed. "Who?" I cry out, before realizing it can only be my mother, come because I must have cried out, because I was frightened. Before I can say anything, she holds up her hand.

"Listen!" she whispers hoarsely. "Can you hear them?" She cocks her head, her finger in the air like a marker. I listen, but hear only the rain. "The feral cats," she says. "They're crying. They want to come in."

Part III

GHOSTS

Camel

—*May 1978*

When *I was a child,* no more than four or five, my parents took me to the Wanango County Fair in Tyler. My father went along grudgingly—then as now, he disliked frivolities. Mrs. Mayhew, our neighbor and my mother's friend and bowling teammate, accompanied us. Her son Bobby was ten years old and could go to the Fair by himself, with friends of his. One night he ran by my bedroom window draped in a sheet, shrieking and wailing and scaring me mightily. He also helped bury my turtle when it got strange spots and died. He was a spirited boy with a sense of fairness as fresh as sunshine, who was to die as a teenager in an auto accident on the French River Road; his mother would follow him in death, of a stroke, only a few months later.

But that was years away, the world had just begun, and

it was the Fair! And it's strange. Although I can easily forget the name of somebody I met just a few hours ago, or what I had for dinner last night, or what happened in the movie I liked so much last week, so that Jena often pronounced me the most forgetful person she knew, even accused me of *wanting* to forget, I remember so much about that Fair—whether those memories were of that one day or of all subsequent fairs I went to, all of them seeming to happen in one long summer afternoon amid the aroma of peanuts and scorched hot dogs and sour lemonade, the churchly smell of suntan lotion and cheap cologne, the dusky, naked odors of straw and livestock.

There were so many wonders! The trained-animal show in which two scrawny dogs leaped desultorily through hoops and over bars and a monkey swung on a rope to land on the clown-trainer's shoulders; the Paradise Bird Show, in which miraculous birds—parrots and macaws and toucans with strange tusky beaks—shimmied and preened and chortled. At the end of the show, to the accompaniment of a scratchy record of march tunes, a peacock stepped lordly into the ring. He surveyed us all with a harsh, judgmental eye and strolled around the perimeter, moving at last to the center, and ever, ever so slowly fanning his tail.

"Ah," my mother said, enchanted.

"Pea hen," my father snorted.

Outside, near the animal judging area, a lady aerialist balanced from the top of a swaying pole on her head, on her hands, on *one* hand. The pole seemed to go as high as the sky, so that she could touch the clouds—even, if she wanted, touch God. Music played for her too, although I wasn't sure she could hear it, she was so high, so far beyond us.

Everything was marvelous! There were the dark tents, dimly lit by strings of twenty-five-watt bulbs, where the grange exhibits were held. These were organized around themes such as PATRIOTISM, AGRICULTURE, FAMILY. The CULTURE exhibit featured a dented trumpet, its polish blistered and tarnished; an open poetry book; an art reproduction from a magazine, clipped out and pasted on a crude cardboard frame. For the ANIMAL HUSBANDRY exhibit someone had arranged a tableau, undoubtedly culled from children's toy boxes, of cloth dolls and plastic figurines of cows and horses and sheep. And more: a monkey doll clung from a raffia vine, a plastic lion hid behind a shock of corn, a stuffed parrot, its feathers half-molted away, perched on a wooden block. What were all these animals doing together on a supposed model of a western Pennsylvania farm? It never occurred to me to wonder.

Corn dogs, Sno-Cones, popcorn, vinegar-and-salt French fries, burned onions, dark Dutch fudge and pralines and peanut-covered candy apples . . .

And the games: Baseball, Gunball, Garbage-Can Ball, Bowlerball, the Balloon Break, the Duck Shoot, the Turtle Pull, Ring-Around-the-Bottle, Penny-in-a-Cup—all manned by two kinds of barkers, the friendly ones, who kept up a stream of patter, encouraging all to come try *(Only a dime a chance—Not much money to win the love of your honey—If you don't win, you can still grin, but it's more fun if you've won)*, or the lean, sullen ones, with tattoos and sideburns, who rarely said anything, content to chew their lips and take your money. They seemed disappointed if you won, and handed over the prizes reluctantly, with a sneer.

And the rides: the Bug, its open cars whipping over the rails with a harsh, scratching sound, like sandpaper blocks rubbed together; the merry-go-round with its prancing music-mirrors that bounced sunlight against our skin so it seemed we were riding our wooden horses through a haze of shimmering silver motes; the Whip, which whooshed and whizzed, so that just standing near it, I could feel the metallic rush of blood to my head; the Hell-Hole, a dark tunnel into which you rode on a small car. Looking into its black maw, clutching my mother's hand, I felt I'd glimpsed something of the power and temptation of Darkness.

At the end of the rides parents and children and teenagers clutching one another would get off, and those watching them would cheer, as if they'd come back from a long and dangerous voyage, and indeed, many did seem to me different now, transfigured and transformed.

We went on all of them, my mother and Mrs. Mayhew whooping and clutching each other and me, my father patiently waiting for us at the gate. We ate hot dogs and caramel corn, and played a few games. My father won a penguin salt-and-pepper set for my mother, and she kissed him. I threw a dart and hit a balloon. It popped, much louder than I would've expected, and I started, and my mother and Mrs. Mayhew laughed.

At the very end of the fairground, we found the camel. Rides were offered for twenty-five cents, and if you wanted your picture taken on it with an old view-camera, that was fifty cents extra. The camel was gaunt, the color of an old carpet, its skin abraded from too many rubbings of saddle and post. Its trainer was an old man in faded denim pants, a ribbed sweater, and, even though it was July, a turban. He had a handlebar mustache and grizzled, unshaven cheeks. I wondered whether he was a pirate, and thought he must be very hot with that turban on. He was assisted by a young boy, barefoot and in shorts. After the man hissed and tapped the camel on the side with a stick to make it kneel, the boy's job was to run out and place a footstool down to help the rider step up and into the saddle. Once the rider was mounted, the boy whisked the stool away, ran back to the camera, and got under the hood. "Hip-hip," the trainer said, and the camel slowly, dutifully rose. The man raised his stick aloft. "Hip-hip-hooray," he'd say and grin sharkily, and the boy would snap the picture. Then the man led camel and rider on a slow turn around the infield, where in the evening the dog races were run. People laughed and bantered and hooted. When the camel returned, the boy once more ran out with the footstool, and the rider dismounted to applause and cheers. In between rides the camel chewed from a pile of hay, its mouth working like those of the tobacco-chewing old men who sat on the park benches near the fountain in Tyler. Every now and then it would spit, just like they did. It hardly seemed to notice us at all, and when it did, its baleful eyes regarded us without interest and with a trace of contempt.

Looking at it made me uneasy. It was big, certainly, but big animals hadn't frightened me before—already I'd ridden the old sorrel horse at my Aunt Ginny's farm and patted a cow. It was ugly, yes, and strange, but that didn't account for my uneasiness either. After all, I'd seen pictures of camels before in my coloring books, and in the *Big Book of Animals* I'd gotten for my birthday. No, it was something about the way it looked at us, as if it knew something we didn't, and would never deign to tell us. Its gaze was cold, without interest or pity, and I felt if I stared into its eyes, I would see nothing, no soul there to stare back.

My mother asked if I'd like to ride the camel. I shook my head vigorously. "I don't want to," I said.

"But why not? Everyone's riding the camel."

"Go on, Frankie," Mrs. Mayhew said. "It'd make such a cute picture. It's a once-in-a-life kind of thing." Mrs. Mayhew liked to see occasions as once-in-life opportunities. "This is a once-in-a-life sale," she'd tell my mother over the phone, or, about some gossip she'd heard, "You'll never hear anything like this again."

"Come on, Frank," my mother urged. She opened her purse for the seventy-five cents for the ride and photo.

"I don't *like* the camel," I cried.

My mother laughed. "Well, why not?"

"It looks like a perfectly good camel to me," Mrs. Mayhew said.

"I don't *like* it," I insisted.

"You're scared of an old, flea-bitten camel?" my father said. "He's not going to hurt you."

"There's no reason to be scared," my mother said. "It's just an old camel."

I furiously shook my head.

"Well, that's the craziest damn thing," my father said. "Scared of a camel."

I felt my lip quiver, and that I might cry.

"Well, if Frank doesn't want to ride," my mother said, "we won't make him."

"Why don't *you* go, Helen?" Mrs. Mayhew suggested. "Show him it's all right."

"Oh, not me," my mother said. "I've got bad luck with animals. When I was a little girl a horse stepped on my ankle and broke it."

"Really!"

"I was just standing there, too. Holding the bridle."

"Go on, Helen," my father said. "We'll get a picture."

"Yes, go on," Mrs. Mayhew said. "Show little Frank there's nothing to be afraid of."

Despite my mother's protestations, they egged her on, and good-naturedly she gave in. The camel returned, and a young girl with a ponytail and halter top jumped off, not even waiting for the footstool. She was met by her shambling boy-friend, who dutifully held two large sticky cotton candies. "Next?" the trainer said softly, a hiss almost. My mother glanced around and saw that she was next. Almost shyly, she stepped forward. She looked at us, gave a resigned shrug, and walked, head down, fists slightly clenched, toward the camel, who watched her with its same indifferent stare. She looked purpose-ful: this was something she had been asked to do and she would do it, endure it, as well as she could. She would ride the camel.

Everything happened just as before: the trainer hissed, the camel knelt, the boy solemnly put down the footstool and helped my mother mount. She sat on the beast, mouth tight, eyes wide, as if afraid it might suddenly rear and race off. I felt my stomach flip-flop a little. *How brave she is,* I thought.

And then the turbaned man chuck-chucked, and the camel rose. My mother was jolted back and gasped in surprise, but held tightly to the reins. I think I might have gasped too. The boy dashed back to the camera. She waved to us, her other hand clutching the reins, as if to show that everything was really all right. *How must we look from her height?* I wondered. Did we now seem small and insignificant? I swallowed. She seemed so far away. The trainer raised his stick and cried, "Hip-hip-hooray, U.S.A.!" and the boy snapped the picture. And then my mother seemed to shrug, assenting to what, I didn't know. She pursed her lips, waved again, and was off. The turbaned man silently led her away, down the track, the camel's footsteps soft as silence. Before I realized that I hadn't waved back, she was gone.

I watched her go away on the camel.

I started to cry. "What's the matter?" my father asked. "What's wrong now?"

"I d-don't *want* her to go!"

"Oh stop crying," he said impatiently. "She'll be back."

And I knew that, I did know that she'd be back, but that didn't assuage the desolation I felt, whose strangeness only confused and frightened me and made me cry harder. And thirty years later, at the reception in Tyler after my mother's funeral, family and strangers around me, all of it—the Fair, that summer afternoon, the camel—came back to me with an intensity that made me dizzy even though I was sitting down, and I realized that I had been weeping then for what had happened now, had been weeping then as I could not weep now, and that even then I was beginning to grieve for her. Even then, our lives together barely begun, I was already learning to say good-bye.

Ghosts

—October 1981

"Oh *my, look* at that one," Jena says, touching my arm. She points to a goblin with a long beaked nose, monster claws, and a Superman cape. He's shuffling along in oversized rubber monster feet—every two steps he has to take a little skip just to keep up with the other ghosts and fairies and witches and cowboys as they, and the occasional adult holding their hand, press resolutely down the street. Jena and I finished lunch— we've been packing and boxing at the house all morning—left the restaurant, turned the corner, and just stumbled on this parade. We haven't even realized that today is Halloween. To us, it's just the day before the first of November, the target date to be moved out of the house, which we've finally sold. I've come back from Michigan to sign papers and help Jena sort out the last stuff; she's already rented an apartment in Redondo Beach, maybe to be near a boyfriend. I don't know, and I've told myself I don't care.

I never realized there were so many kids in town. It seems like there are hundreds of them, bunched and scrunched together in their masks and costumes, shuffling along God knows where in a zombie conga line. Who organized the damn thing I have no idea, but it's cute and it's funny, so Jena and I sit on the curb to watch for a while.

"That cowboy's britches are going to fall down," I say, nudging her. She squints behind her sunglasses and grins. It's true, the little boy is having a hard time—the belt of his gun holster isn't cinched tight enough, and he looks panicky, a desperado desperately looking for help.

"Poor little kid," Jena says. "I should go tighten him up." But she doesn't. He hitches his pants again and shambles on. Two twins dressed as bullfrogs hop by, making burping sounds. A spaceman with an eerily whining death ray zaps them and half the audience, too. A little girl walks by in a bride's outfit, complete with miniature bouquet of plastic flowers.

"That's obscene," Jena says.

"Maybe it's a Communion dress or something," I say.

"I don't care. It's still obscene. That's not what Halloween's all about."

I'm going to ask her just what it is all about, then, if not masks and costumes, but she touches my arm and says, "Which one do you think is ours?"

I don't know what she's talking about.

"If you could pick any of these kids to be ours," she says, "which one would it be?" She's looking at me mischievously, something of the old lilt in her voice, and I get a little catch in my throat and a skip in my stomach.

"That's a really strange question, Jena," I say. "I mean, none of them could be our kid."

"I know that," she says. "I'm just asking you to *imagine.*"

I point randomly. "That one."

"That bug? That *roach?*" She stares at a plumpish kid in a yellow-and-black-striped insect costume. He has a conical tail—a stinger of sorts—and a cap with antennae on elastic coils which bob and knock about like crazy plant stalks.

"He's a bumblebee, I think," I tell her.

Jena studies him as he passes. "That surprises me."

"Why? Don't you see the stinger?"

"I mean, that you'd pick him to be our kid. I thought for sure you'd pick some little girl, some little daisy or princess or something."

I'm looking at a tall, beautiful woman who's very delicately holding the hand of a little girl in a witch's costume. It's velveteen, and looks handmade, the cape fastened with a small gold brooch, the cap carefully cut and stapled together with felt around the brim. The woman walks regally, her eyes sad, a queen among her elfin subjects. I think how beautiful she is, how much love she must have to make her daughter such a costume. I think how she should have been the woman I married.

"They need music," I say. "There's no music in this parade."

"There's no such thing as Halloween music, Frank."

"The worms crawl in, and the worms crawl out . . ." I sing in a slow Transylvanian drawl.

Jena laughs.

". . . the worms crawl in and around your snout." I scrunch my lips, wrinkle my nose, and move closer to her neck, as if I'm going to nuzzle her. She wears her hair much shorter now, and I'm not used to the almost bare skin around her nape.

She leans back. "Don't," she says, giggling, and when I come at her once more, cackling, she says again, "Don't." She rises, brushes off her jeans, and starts walking back to the car, hands in her pockets, head down.

BACK AT THE HOUSE, all the heavy furniture is already gone: Jena had some student movers come and take what she wanted to her new apartment. Some pieces that neither of us have room for—like the antique sideboard we bought at an estate sale in San Bernardino—we're putting in storage until one of us really settles down again. Wardrobe boxes with Jena's clothes line the wall. The oak floors need buffing, I see, but the new owners will do that, not us—it's their headache now. With all the furniture and rugs and pictures gone, I would've thought the rooms would look larger, but they don't.

The task at hand is to clean out the odds and ends— clothes and unused kitchen stuff and camping gear and maga- zines, the detritus of a marriage—that have accumulated in the back bedroom, the one we used as a storeroom. Everything we didn't need we pitched back there, until the place looked like a junk shop. Every other month Jena used to say we should clean it out, that rats and roaches and beetles and God knows what could be breeding back there, but like so many other things, we never got around to it.

We're dividing things into three piles: stuff I want, stuff Jena wants, and stuff for Goodwill, who're coming by this eve- ning. There's very little in the first two piles, much more in the third. It's easier just to throw things out, it seems, rather than decide what to keep. "Don't you want that?" Jena asks, as I put a badminton set on the Goodwill pile.

"Why? Where am I going to play badminton?"

"You never know, honey. We'll all have other lives."

"One thing you can count on," I say. "I won't be playing badminton there."

She turns on the portable radio to a golden-oldies station. *Sugar, sugar,* the Archies sing, *Oh honey, honey.* I pick up a canteen, a relic from our brief backpacking days. The canvas cover is rotting away, revealing the dull aluminum underneath. For a moment I wonder whether I should save it—you never know when you're going to be stranded somewhere and need water—but then I throw it away, too. I take the Goodwill stuff out to the large pile outside the door. They told us they'd box it themselves, since they had to make a list for our receipt.

"I meant to ask you," Jena says when I return. "How's your father doing?"

"He's handling things okay, I guess." It's been over three years now since my mother died. "He misses Mom a lot, you know."

She nods.

My father loved Jena, and I think he, even more than my mother, was hurt by our splitting. He'd always told me that marrying her was the best thing I'd ever done, that I really lucked out there. Since we separated, he hasn't really known what to say about her to me, nor how to ask about us, so he and I have both kept a cautious, tender silence about it all.

"Did you ever send him a card?" I ask. "After Mom died?"

She puts down the box of Christmas ornaments she's been sorting through. "Now why do you ask that?"

"I just never heard him say anything about it."

"Well, I didn't. I'm sorry." Jena shakes her head. "I'm bad about those things."

"Jesus, it's just a *card,* Jen."

"I just don't know what to say to people who are grieving, Frank. When I was a kid, Sarah Goodall next door had an Easter chick that died, and when she told me, I burst out laughing."

She winces. "It wasn't like I was *glad* or anything. Just . . . nervous." She looks at me. "Why do we do things like that?"

The doorbell rings. Jena looks at me as if I'm going to answer it, as if I still lived here too, then gets up and goes. I hear her open the door and talk to somebody. I go to the kitchen, get a beer, and stand in the hallway to catch a look. It's Antonio, the guy who trims the ivy and bushes. Four years since I moved out and she's still using him. Faithfulness.

Jena comes back to the kitchen. "Antonio," she says. "He's come for his last payment." She gets her purse from the window sill and rummages through it. "Jesus, where did I put my checkbook?" Her hand flies to her mouth. "My God, maybe I left it at my apartment!"

I take out my checkbook. "How much?"

"Frank, you don't need to—"

"Hey, let me do this for you," I say. "My pleasure." *Antonio,* I write, and for the date, *Halloween.* "What's his last name?"

"Jesus, I forget. Every month I have to look in my checkbook to see his name from the last check. I just can't seem to remember it." She squinches her lips. "Jesus, this is so embarrassing." She glances back at the doorway, as if Antonio might be overhearing all this.

"I'll go do it," I say. "I'm not supposed to remember."

Antonio looks at me as if I were a ghost. "Hey, mister," he greets me. I realize he can't remember my name either. "You back now?"

"Just visiting."

"Ah." He nods, as if he knew this all the time. He glances at his truck in the drive, where one of his workers sits, a man with a brown, squashed face.

I put my checkbook against the door to write. "What's your last name, Antonio?"

"Herrera." He spells it. He gets asked this a lot, I bet. *Herrera*, I write. Not so hard to remember. Antonio takes the check with a little formal nod.

"You and Missus together again?" He makes a circling motion with his finger, as if togetherness, family, love were all contained within it, and I look, as if I could see them there, too.

"No," I say. "I'm in Michigan. She's moving to Redondo Beach."

He looks around at the ivy, the azaleas, the acacia palms at either corner of the drive. "That one"—he points—"not doing so good." He looks concerned. It occurs to me that Antonio has cared for all this more than me.

"Maybe the new people will want to use you, Antonio. We'll recommend you to them."

He shrugs. He points to the Goodwill pile by the door. "You throwing this out?"

"Yes."

"You want, I take it," he says, not looking at me. "No charge."

"Sure," I say. "Take it. It's all yours."

Antonio waves to the man in the truck and yells something in Spanish. The man gets out, comes over, and starts hauling it all back to the truck—sweaters, plastic plates, mosquito netting, a battery lantern, a cooler with a broken lid, the canteen. Antonio opens up the badminton set, takes out a racket and shuttlecock. "Tennis." He grins, and mimes hitting it. He calls to his friend and waves the racket and shuttlecock. The man laughs. For a moment I think Antonio is going to hit the shuttlecock over to him, maybe start playing badminton right there in the drive, but then he carefully puts racket and shuttlecock back in the box. A few more minutes and everything's loaded.

"See you now," Antonio says to me. "You good customers." And then: "You take care."

"I will. I'll do that." I wave as they pull out of the drive.

Jena is going through boxes of magazines when I come back. "Jesus," she says, "what the hell were you talking about with him?"

"I haven't seen him for a while. We were catching up on things."

"Old buddies, huh?"

"He's an interesting fellow. He likes to go camping. Plays badminton, too."

She looks at me quizzically, then furrows her brow. "You didn't give him—"

I nod.

"Frank, that was for Goodwill!"

"Antonio will use it. It's still goodwill."

She shakes her head. "What's the use of having them come now? That was half the stuff!"

"I'd rather have our things with someone I know. A friend." I say this with more seriousness than I imagined.

Jena smiles. "Are you going to get gloppy and sentimental? Now?"

The doorbell rings again. I hold up my hand. "I'll get it. You just continue the good work."

There's a man there in a white knit shirt, navy Ban-Lon pants. His stomach is creeping over the waistband, and a pack of cigarets bulges from his shirt pocket. Through the thin knit I can see a jersey undershirt. I didn't know men even wore those anymore. He's in his fifties, his hair precisely parted and mashed down—it looks so perfect, I wonder if it's a toupee. His face is florid, the cheeks pockmarked from youthful acne.

"Clive Barrow, Liberty Insurance," he says heartily, thrusting out his hand. As I'm shaking it, he hands me a card with the other, and we do a weird little hand-change shuffle. "I drive by here a lot and I noticed people moving out last week, and then I see your car"—he nods toward my rental car—"and I wondered if maybe you folks were the new owners."

"No," I say. "We're the old owners. We're just cleaning up a few things."

"Ah." He looks disappointed. "I guess I never really saw you here before. How long you live here?"

"Six years."

"How about that? And I drive by here all the time! Why, I live just two streets over. I guess I should've come by sooner, right?" He spreads his arms wide, and for a moment I think he's going to envelop me in a bear hug.

"I never did much lawn work," I say. "We had a gardener."

He looks puzzled.

"So you wouldn't have seen me out in the yard much," I explain.

"Oh. *Oh.*" He presses his palms together. His hands stay busy, I notice. "Well, I just thought I'd drop by and say hello, if you were the new owners. I guess I've said hello anyways." We both look at his card. He seems sorry he's given it to me. "Where you folks moving to?" he asks heartily, as if aware he's been too obvious with his disappointment.

"I've already moved," I say. "We're separated. That was my wife's stuff you saw going out last week."

"Oh." He knits his brow in a studied expression of concern. "Sorry to hear that."

"And we're not getting any new houses."

He holds up his hands. "Oh, look, I don't—"

"I'm a bad risk anyway," I say. "I've got the wrong attitude about houses. As a matter of fact, I'm thinking about burning this one down."

He looks at me blankly.

"Just kidding," I say.

He blinks. Then, almost confidentially, he says, "I know how it is. I went through two of 'em myself." I think for a moment he means house-burnings, but then realize he's talking about divorces, and he means it as some sort of consolation. "You've gotta stand tall," he says. "That's half of it right there." As if to demonstrate, he squares his shoulders slightly. "Well . . ." He goes down a step, then points to the door. "You really ought to get deadbolts, you know. Those spring locks aren't worth diddly. You tell the next people about that."

"You can tell them yourself," I say good-naturedly.

He laughs. "Maybe I will. I'll drop by sooner, that's for sure." He waves. "Well, good luck."

Everybody's wishing me good luck today.

"Who was that?" Jena asks. She's sitting on the floor taking a break, beer can balanced on one knee. I sit down across from her and lean back against the wall.

"Insurance salesman," I say.

"Jesus. What a time to call."

"I don't think he's very successful." Now that I've said it, I feel genuinely sorry for Clive Barrow. I touch my shirt pocket—his card's still there. I'm going to remember all their names, I decide. Antonio Herrera. Clive Barrow.

"I was having lunch with Carmen yesterday." Jena takes a swig of beer, wipes her forehead. "She told me the weirdest story."

Inwardly, I wince. Jena has a way of telling stories, unraveling them slowly, yarn by yarn, that can drive me nuts. Most of the time they don't seem to have a moral, or a point, or a punch line, and I'll be sitting there nodding impatiently, my mind glazing.

"She works in a law office over on Foothill. You know, in that professional building? Well, evidently one of the lawyers there got a phone call the other day. It was late, no one else in the office, and he gets this call from some guy who said he was in another state, and he wanted some legal advice. The guy tells him his wife is very sick, cancer or something, and he's having problems with their health insurance, they won't pay for some kind of treatment she needs, and—"

"Wait a minute. Why'd this guy call him from another state? Health insurance is different in each state."

She holds up her hand. "Wait. You'll see. So the lawyer talks to him, and tries to get the details of the case, but the guy's not really forthcoming, you know, he won't say exactly where he lives, won't give any names, and the lawyer is thinking something's funny, but still there's real panic in the guy's voice, he seems sincere—"

"So what happened?" I ask, hurrying her along.

"They talk some more. And then this guy breaks down and starts sobbing, just bawling, saying how afraid he is of his wife dying, how he just doesn't know what he's going to do if she does. He's so scared. And now the lawyer gets the feeling there's really no problem with the medical insurance at all, or if there is, it's not much of one, and that this guy's really just called to talk."

"Why call him?"

Again she holds up her hand, signaling patience. "So the lawyer talks to him awhile, tells him maybe he should get some counseling, and the guy says, well, how could he afford that, would his insurance pay for that too? Not likely. He's still crying like a baby. So the lawyer tries to calm him down a bit, reassure him, and, you know, get him off the phone. Which eventually he does."

"Nothing like the compassion of lawyers," I say.

She looks at me. "I think he was very compassionate. He talked to him a long time, after all."

A truck rumbles by, shaking the house. They aren't supposed to use our street, but sometimes they go through anyway, since it cuts a few blocks off getting to the freeway.

"But that's not the important thing," Jena says. "That's not the real end of the story." She looks at me, a child with a secret.

"So what's the real end?"

"Peter—this lawyer—hangs up and leaves the office to go home. His office is in that professional building, you know, and they've got other offices there too. Now it's late, remember, everybody's gone home. But as he's going by the office right down the hall, he glances through the window—they've got those big hallway picture windows—and he sees a guy sitting in a cubicle, all the lights off except for his. He's got one hand on a phone, another shading his eyes, and for a moment Peter thinks he's asleep, dozing or something, and then he realizes the guy's shoulders are trembling, shaking. He's crying." She looks at me. "It may have been the same guy," she says, as if I didn't get it. "He was just calling from down the hall."

"Peter didn't know him?"

She shakes her head.

"Then it doesn't really matter, does it?" I say. "Whether he was in Oshkosh or just down the hall. Same thing, isn't it?"

"You don't get it, do you? You don't see how . . . how *sad* it all is." She shakes her head in exasperation. "There's something really sad there." She stands up and starts ruffling through a pile of dresses. "Just forget it, okay? There's no use telling you any stories."

"I tell you what's sad," I say. "Carmen didn't tell you this at all, did she? This is Peter who told you this. Right? One of your boyfriends?"

She starts throwing dresses, blouses, skirts onto the new Goodwill pile, not even looking at them.

"It wasn't Carmen, was it?"

"Oh, stop it! Jesus, what does it matter?"

"Was it?"

"It *was!*"

One of the dresses in the Goodwill pile catches my eye and I go over and pick it up. I feel my neck flush. "Jena—" I hold up the tailored dress, navy blue with a white trim collar. "My mother gave you this dress." Underneath it on the pile, I see a challis two-piece dress, another gift from my mother. She'd give Jena things of hers—scarves and blouses and skirts, things she'd hardly worn—when we visited at Christmas. "You're not throwing these out, are you?"

"I don't want them, Frank." She doesn't look at me.

"Jena—" I hold out the dress, as if she didn't see clearly. "This was my mother's. She gave it to you. It was *hers.*"

"It doesn't fit right, Frank. Your mother was thicker-waisted than me. I don't know why she kept giving me stuff anyway.

"You can get it *altered,* for Christ's sake—"

"I don't want to get it altered." She tosses the beach towels we got on a vacation in Carmel onto the pile, as if to cover up the other dress.

"But you *liked* this dress. I remember you saying—"

"Frank, I never liked that dress. I just said I did so I wouldn't hurt her feelings. What else could I say? I *hate* that dress."

"You *can't* throw it away! It's my mother's!"

"Well, you take it then." She waves her hand.

"How can you do that?" My voice feels as if it'll crack. "How can you just throw away . . . I mean . . . what she—"

"Frank." Her voice is conciliatory, almost pleading. "Your mother's taste and mine were just one hundred and eighty degrees apart. Where she got the idea her clothes looked good on me—"

"It's *her* you didn't like, isn't it?"

"God, Frank—"

"All that time in the hospital . . . " I throw the dress down. "All that time she was sick, you never *once* called, never *once* sent a card . . . "

She sits down again, folds her arms around her knees.

"What about that book you were going to send her?" I demand. "What about *that?*"

"Don't, Frank. Please."

"All that time. Nothing!" I point, shake my finger. "She was dead to you way before she died."

She holds up a hand, as if to stanch my words.

"And nothing to my father! My God, he *loved* you, Jena! And you never even sent him a card. One little *card!* Jesus, it's—it's—just *incredible.*"

Jena is silent, staring out the door, down the hall, somewhere farther, away.

"Well, say something, goddammit!"

"What?" She looks at me, eyes glistening. "You want me to say I was wrong? Okay—I was wrong. I'm a bad person. What else?"

I pick up the dress. "Here." I toss it at her. It lands at her feet. "Put it on!"

She stares at me.

"I just want to see," I say. "I want to see if it really looks that bad on you."

"Frank, Frank—"

"Put it on!" I think she won't, but she picks up the dress and puts it on her lap, smoothing it out. Then she slowly gets up, as if her bones ache. She looks at me, and pulls her tee over her head. She's not wearing a bra, and her breasts swing loose and free. The ease with which she does this, when I haven't seen her naked for years, startles me. She unzips her jeans. I feel the ghost of old desires, old loves, stirring like leaves in an attic, and it scares me, it's nothing I want to feel. She looks at me, then steps out of her jeans. I go to the window and look out on the patio. The pink-and-white bushes—I forget their name—are in full bloom. Antonio's taken good care of them, too.

"All right," Jena says, and I turn. Her hands are folded primly, as if we were very young and this were a first date. She's right, the dress is too long, way too big in the waist and shoulders, and the colors don't go well with her reddish-blond hair. She looks at once forlorn and defiant, caught between trying to please and wanting to escape, and I feel ashamed.

"Okay," I say, "you've made your point." And because I can't say anything else, I go down the hall, and out the front door. I get in my car and sit. My thoughts are tumbling around, swirling like dead leaves. I start driving, just to do something, to go somewhere.

A couple miles down Foothill, I see one of those little carnivals that sprout like mushrooms in shopping centers, and I pull in. I get out and walk around. Lights, already on in the dusk, are threaded in long peppery strings around the parking lot. They've got a Ferris wheel, a carousel with badly chipped horses turning to music that sounds like it was recorded under the sea, and a Wild Mouse whose cars, despite its name, roll lugubriously up and down a gently humped track. There's a little train, too, with recorded sound effects—*"All aboard!"* and whistles and chugging and tooting. The bell on the locomotive is real, however, and the "engineer"—a thin, pimply-faced young man—sporadically yanks it. Because it's Halloween, there's a fun house, too, the Creepy Castle, a canvas structure rigged over a plywood-and-metal skeleton. Creaturely groans and moans emanate from within. An inflatable rubber bridge connects the Castle's two bastions. People enter, then reappear a little while later, giggling and shrieking, to stumble across the bridge. The adults walk gingerly, hands on the guideropes, eyes on the other side, while the kids, heedless and cheerful, jump up and down, not caring whether they fall or tumble or roll. It doesn't matter how or when they get across, they just seem to have faith they will, so why not have fun doing it? Then they disappear again into the Castle, never to come out. *The exit must be in the rear,* I think.

I find a pay phone, call Goodwill, and tell them not to come, that we've got nothing to give them after all. "Will you have it tomorrow?" the woman asks in a nasal voice. I tell her no, not then either. We're keeping everything, I say.

I drive back to the house. It's full dusk now, deep and coral and amethyst. Rather than go in the front, I go around to the patio. I can hear Fleetwood Mac singing "Come a Little Bit Closer" on the radio. The light's on in the bedroom and the curtains are gone, so it's easy to look in. Jena, back in her jeans again, is dancing. Her eyes are closed, and she's swaying to the music, her hips softly undulating, shoulders rising and falling like water. She is lovely in the light and in the music, like a swimmer almost, lovely and alone. I think, *I have never seen this before.* And I wonder if all the time we were married, she'd secretly been dancing by herself, and I'd never known. If I had—if I'd taken her in my arms and just danced with her—would it have made any difference? Would she have even wanted me to? Or was this for her alone, her passion and her secret?

In all the world, I think, there's nothing so strange as the soul of someone you live with. Because you think you know everything about them, you see nothing. After five minutes of talking with him, I probably knew more about Clive Barrow, insurance salesman, than I would ever know about Jena.

I walk around to the front and go in. When I go back to the bedroom, Jena is sealing a box, no sign at all that she'd been dancing. I want to take her in my arms and say I'm sorry. *I saw you dancing,* I want to say, *and I'm just so sorry.*

"I want to tell you something," she says. She puts down the tape and scissors.

"Okay," I say.

"You're right, I never sent your father a card." She pauses. "But I did visit him once."

I sit down on one of the packing boxes. "What do you mean?"

"Last Christmas, when I went back to visit my folks, I made a trip over to Tyler to see him."

I'm flabbergasted. "He never told me about this."

She pulls her knees to her chest. "I didn't really *plan* to go see him. But maybe because I was so close, and I'd been feeling, you know, so guilty over not sending a card or anything, and never getting in touch with your mother when she was sick . . . " She looks at me, her face suddenly anguished. "I *did* feel guilt, dammit! It's not like you've been thinking. It was just"—she makes a motion with her hands, as if trying to grasp smoke, or water—"so *hard.* We'd split up, and I didn't know what my . . . my relation was somehow . . ." She stops for a moment.

"And then it got worse. Like to say *anything* would only make it worse, because I was so late saying it. But when I was back last Christmas, I thought one morning, okay, just do it. So I drove up to Tyler. I didn't call him or anything, because I really

didn't know if I'd go through with it or not when I got there.
I—"

"Wait a minute," I say. "Weren't you worried that I
might be there? I mean, Christmas . . ."

She shakes her head. "I knew you were in Michigan.
Jillian"—a friend of ours who occasionally calls me up to make
strained conversation—"told me."

"Good old Jillian."

She's quiet, and I wonder if she's going to say any more,
that maybe she thinks that's it. "So what happened?" I ask.
"When you saw Dad?"

"He was very sweet. We had dinner. I told him how sorry
I was, how bad I felt. I told him I should've written, but I'd
. . . I'd been . . . nervous. And afraid. I was getting confused
trying to explain it. He said it was okay. Frank, he's *much* more
understanding than you give him credit for. And then he started,
you know, getting teary, his voice breaking as he talked about
your mother, and—and I got the strangest panicky feeling. Like
I wanted to jump up and run away. And then I realized I was
still afraid. And that was what I was afraid of."

I look at her, not understanding.

"Grief," she said. "I'm afraid of grief."

"Grief? His grief?"

"Mine, Frank." She closes her eyes, and when she opens
them again, it's as if she's looking through me, a ghost. "Do you
understand?"

"I don't know." My head feels light, floating.

She wraps her arms around her knees. "We had dinner
and went back to your house. I thought I'd just leave—it was
late, and I was still feeling strange, you know. But he told me
I should stay there the night, it was too late to drive back
anyway. Besides, he said, it would be nice to have someone in

the house. Since you didn't come back very much." She looks at me. "So I did."

Outside, I can hear crickets. The next-door neighbor's sprinkler comes on. Somewhere, a child is yelling, "I can't see you, can't see you, can't see you."

"That's all?"

"What more should there be, Frank?"

I feel a tightening in my throat.

"You think we slept together or something? We didn't."

"Jena, I—"

"Oh, there was a moment when we might've," she says. "We were standing at the bottom of the stairs. He'd just given me blankets and sheets for the guest room, and he had the saddest look on his face, as if I were going to go away and leave him too, and it hit me, just right then, that he really was alone, not just for a few days or anything, but every day. It was like, what did my own problems, my . . . my selfish little ego, matter, you know? I just felt so selfish. I kissed him on the cheek, and he put his hands on my shoulders. I moved closer, and he held me, and maybe we kissed again, I don't remember. And then we just sort of pulled away, and said good night. I left the next morning."

I feel my heart go cold, a numbness come over my body. Dying must be like this, I think, the bleeding of the soul of all warmth, all love, a seepage of the spirit as much as flesh. There will be nothing between us now, I think—no secrets, yes, but nothing else either. Between us will be vast expanses, steppes of silence, distances too far to call from . . .

"So," I say. "There it is."

"Yes. Such as it is." Jena studies my face. "I shouldn't have told you this, should I?"

"Oh no. I'm *glad* you told me. Now I know, right?"

"I'm always saying the wrong thing," she says. She raises her hand, lets it fall. "Whatever I tell you, it's wrong. I'm always too late, or too early, or whatever." She laughs bitterly. "I just can't get my timing down."

The silence between us is thick and stale, the silence of empty closets and closed rooms. It is too painful to attend, so I listen to the evening, crickets, traffic. A neighbor's sprinkler turns off. A thumping on the roof—a branch or something has fallen from the live-oak tree. One night a raccoon climbed down that tree and scratched against our bedroom window, frightening us half to death. When I turned on the light, he didn't run away at all, but kept scraping, nose pressed to the window like a curious child, as if he wanted to come in.

Jena stands, picks up a pile of clothes. They seem to weigh heavily in her arms. She walks down the hall to the front room.

"I spoke to Goodwill," I call after her. "I told them not to bother coming." She doesn't seem to hear.

I stand there, my mind racing, then growing strangely blank, so blank I can't think of words, I can't think of names, I can't think at all. I follow Jena. "I want to tell you something," I say.

She turns and looks at me, the clothes held tight against her chest.

And just like in the movies when the action rises to a pitch or the pauses grow pregnant, the doorbell rings. Jena and I stare, as if each expected the other to explain who might still be out there to call on us, darkness and evening having come. For the last time in my house, I answer the door.

They are little kids, one in a goblin's costume, the other dressed like a pirate, with bandana and paper mustache and black cork around the eyebrows. Just little kids, and I can't tell if they are boys or girls or what. I have the strangest feeling they could be anybody's kids, ours even, come home with the evening's booty. "Trick or treat!" the pirate yells, and giggles. And I can't say anything, my voice, like a bobbed apple, just sticks in my throat. "We don't have anything to give you," I finally say. As if they won't believe me, I turn to one side so they can see the half-empty house, the boxes, all the piles of last things, and Jena standing there, as if waiting for someone to come and take her away also. "As you can see," I say, my voice oddly formal, as if I were a tour guide and these not little children at all, but some judges come to our door in the night, "no one lives here anymore at all."

Summer People

—September 1983

Frank and his father drove up to the lake at the end of the season, not long after the summer people—including those who had rented the house—had returned to their real homes, taking with them their grills and motorboats and deck chairs and water skis. It was a mid-September morning. A milky haze—the ghost of an earlier fog—hung over the lake, and the trees loomed grayish-green, half-water, half-air. Geese honked from somewhere within. His father parked on the dead grass behind the summer house.

"Well, we're here," he announced.

Neither of them moved to get out. Frank sipped the coffee, already lukewarm, that they'd bought down at the turnoff, at the Mini-Mart. His father rolled down the window and breathed deeply. "Chilly," he said.

"It'll warm up," Frank said.

The blue spruce and pine surrounding the house seemed larger than Frank remembered, while the house itself seemed smaller. He realized—and was surprised—that he was still taking their measure from childhood memories. He closed his eyes, as if to finally dissolve them, and looked again. *It's time to see things as they are,* he told himself.

His father had recently repainted the house the same light green as always, although Frank remembered the shutters as white, not brown. "I'm going to repaint it," he'd told Frank in a phone call earlier that summer. "And then I'm going to sell it."

"Do you really want to do that?" Frank asked.

"It's not worth the trouble of keeping it up anymore, Frank. I don't go there, what with your mother gone. And I'm tired of renting it. All I do is worry about it all summer." He paused. "And you never use it."

In July his father had called again. "Well, I think I've sold it."

"That's good," Frank said.

"They're a real nice family. They've got a boy about the age you were when we first went up there."

And still later, in mid-August, his father surprised Frank by asking him to come help close up the house for the season.

"Dad, why? I'm three hundred miles away. What happened to that boy you get to help you?"

"I want to do a real good job for these new people." His father cleared his throat. "Besides, we don't see each other much anymore."

Frank said nothing.

"It's the last year," his father said. "Please."

Frank hesitated, then agreed.

"But I don't want to argue," he said. "No arguments."

"Not from me," his father reassured him.

Across the lake the geese skirred the water, flew into the mist, and vanished. His father opened the car door and threw the last of his coffee on the ground, where it steamed. "Well, it's a good day for doing it," he said. "Last year it was hot as hell."

While his father unlocked the cellar to find the tools they'd need, Frank walked, hands in pockets, to the dock and stared into the mist. Wavelets lapped the pilings. A foamy scum of decaying leaves and algae ringed the bank, which curved in close by the dock to form a small cove. Frank lay on his stomach, as he'd done as a child, and dipped his hand into the water. Cold as ever. He sat up. He looked across the water and saw winter, snow, the lake frozen over and two small figures skating in the dark. They are he and Jena, and they are skating away from each other. What had they been arguing about that evening? Frank had forgotten.

He did not want to be here. Here was the past, a place Frank disliked visiting. As the years went by, more and more people he knew seemed to have gone there, descended into its mists and shadowed valleys, never to return. No messages could be sent there, and none came out. All that was left of his own time there were images, memories like blank postcards with no captions, nothing to remind him of the color of the days, or how he'd passed the time, or why he had even been there.

We'll just close the place quickly, he told himself, *and then we can go.*

Frank saw the rope dangling from the huge oak that jutted out over the cove. "I'll be damned," he murmured. He heard his father come up behind him. Frank pointed. "That's the rope swing. The one you used to tell me not to swing from."

His father squinted. "So it is."

"Jesus, I can't believe it's still there. Why hasn't it rotted away?"

"It's heavy rope," his father said. "Oiled."

It had been here the times he'd come before, Frank thought, and he'd never noticed it. The rope fell from the higher branches past a large limb some thirty feet above the water. That had been the jumping-off point. As a boy, Frank had climbed there on the boards someone had nailed into the trunk. Barefoot on the rough bark, he'd grasped the rope in defiance of his father and stared down at the water which stared back at him, dark and judgmental and waiting.

"I never understood why you didn't want me to jump from there," Frank said.

His father shrugged. "It was your mother. She was afraid you'd hit your head on one of the lower branches. Or hit the water wrong."

"I did it anyway, you know. When you weren't around." Frank stared high into the branches and saw himself poised in the gooseflesh moment before flight, before the abandonment to gravity, to water, to faith. "I was scared, but I did it."

His father grunted.

"It wasn't that high," Frank said.

They walked back to the house. His father took a key from his ring and turned the lock. He jiggled the key, pulled hard on the knob, turned it again. "Damn lock gets worse every year," he muttered. He jiggled the key harder, and the door opened. "I've got to replace it."

"Let the other folks worry about it, Dad," Frank said. His father looked puzzled. "I mean, it's not going to be your worry anymore, is it?"

"You've got to take care of things," his father said.

They opened the shades and diffused morning light poured into the front room. The smell of pine and must seemed more pungent than ever to Frank—that and the smell of the lake, raw and brackish, always stronger here than down at the water's edge. The print of *Lake Leman by Moonlight* still hung over the fireplace; the driftwood lamp still adorned the end table. He could see his mother lying on the sofa, hand pressed to her forehead, listening to the radio in the spare and dwindling light. He saw Jena and him sitting by the fireplace, roasting hot dogs and drinking beer while outside the trees creaked in the cold, like old men's bones. It was the first time Jena had been here. How could they know it would also be the only time?

"Still seem the same?" his father asked.

Frank nodded. *Nothing changes*, he thought. *Except everything.*

His father went upstairs to inspect, and Frank walked into the kitchen. The sun had come out now, and its light through the drawn shades tinted the room golden brown. He opened the refrigerator: it was empty, and clean, as were the cupboards. Above him the floorboards creaked as his father walked through rooms opening closet doors, window shutters, bureau drawers. Frank leaned against the sink and looked out the window. Leaves were already starting to fall. He could see his mother slowly raking them, pausing to extend her hand to a skittish orange-and-black cat. Were those cats still under the porch? What had happened to that god-awful dog? What had happened to his mother? To Jena? Why were he and his father the only ones left?

His father came downstairs. "They did a pretty good job cleaning up."

"The kitchen looks good," Frank said.

His father opened the refrigerator, then the freezer.

"They defrosted it," he said in wonder. "On the last season, I finally get some decent renters." He sat down at the kitchen table. "One year people left some Coke bottles in the freezer, and they exploded all over the damn place. Did I ever tell you that?" He picked up a salt shaker and turned it over in his fingers. "Another time, your mother and I found all the porch chairs in the closet, broken up and stacked like kindling. Can you believe that?" He tipped the shaker, and a little salt fell on the table. He carefully swept it into his palm. "People just don't care."

"Maybe we should get started, Dad," Frank suggested.

"What's the hurry? We've got all day." His father unscrewed the top of the shaker and brushed the salt back inside. "Let's take it easy, do a good job, then go have a nice dinner somewhere." He wiped his hands on his pants.

"So, what do you want me to do?" Frank asked.

His father folded his hands. He seemed not to hear.

"Dad?"

"You're not sorry I sold it, are you?"

"The house? Why should I be?"

"You spent a lot of summers here. I just thought you might be sorry to see it go."

"Dad, like you said, I've never used it. It's your place, not mine."

"Your mother and I hoped to keep it in the family, you know. It could've been a place where you and Jena could come and bring your children, but—"

"I know, Dad. No Jena. No kids."

"Well, I just thought I might as well sell it."

"It's okay. Don't worry about it, okay?"

"She never even saw it, did she? Jena?"

"We broke in here once," Frank said.

"You did? When?"

"Years ago. We broke the latch of the window over the sink. You must have fixed it later."

His father went over to the window and looked. He turned the latch back and forth.

"I told you, Dad. It's fixed now."

"You know, I don't remember. Did your mother know about this?"

"No. I never told her."

His father raised the window, then lowered it. He closed the latch and stared out, and kept staring, and suddenly Frank wondered whether he too could see his mother out there.

"Dad? Why don't we get started?" Frank lightly clapped his hands. "What do you want me to do? How about if I drain the hot-water tank?"

"It would've been nice," his father said, "to have other kids here."

Frank tensed. "I'm going to go drain the hot-water tank."

"Do you remember how?" His father turned from the window. "I can show you if you've forgotten."

"I remember, Dad." Frank spoke like a schoolboy reciting a lesson: "Hose out the window, lower than the level of the heater."

"Don't forget to turn it off when you're done."

"I know."

When Frank came up from the cellar with the hose, his father had gone back upstairs. Frank attached one end of the hose to the water-heater spigot, uncoiled it across the floor, and dropped the other end out the window. He turned on the spigot: rust-colored water spluttered, then gurgled steadily onto the ground outside. He wet a sponge and ran it across sink and stove and counters. By the flapping sounds upstairs, he knew his father was covering furniture with sheets and canvas. Frank looked at the grease traps on the stove—clean. He opened the oven. Charred grease rimmed the bottom pan and ridging. *One thing they didn't do,* he thought grimly. *We'll be here all afternoon cleaning this.* He closed the oven door and rechecked the hose. Only a small trickle was coming out now. Frank turned off the water heater, uncoupled the hose, dragged it across the floor, and dumped it out the window. A cardinal with a missing tail feather landed and hopped along its coils, as if inspecting it.

He'll probably ask me if I turned off the heater, Frank thought. He went over and checked it again before going upstairs.

His mother's room was closed. Frank hesitated for a moment, then walked softly by, as if she might still be inside, resting. His father was in Frank's old bedroom, adjusting a sheet to drape over the chest of drawers. He picked up the ship in a bottle Frank had made one summer and held it out to him. "I helped you make this, remember? Remember how you couldn't get the sails to untangle?"

Frank shook his head.

"You got real frustrated. I think you would've given up if I hadn't helped."

"I don't remember," Frank said.

"Do you want to take it?"

Frank shook his head. "You keep it, Dad."

"Well, all right. I will." His father carefully placed it on the bed and draped the sheet over the chest of drawers. "Finished in the kitchen?"

Frank nodded. "I drained the tank and cleaned up a bit."

"How was the oven?"

"Just fine," Frank lied.

"These were *really* good renters," his father said admiringly. "They usually forget that."

"Dad, what happened to the cats?"

"Cats? What cats?"

"The cats that used to live under the porch."

His father frowned. "I don't remember any cats."

"They were here that time I came to check up on Mom. A whole colony living under the porch."

He shook his head. "I never saw any cats."

"But they'd been here every summer for years, she said."

His father shrugged. "Never saw 'em."

Frank was disconcerted. Memory, at times so overpowering, seemed to quickly become smoke and shadow. *They* had *been here,* he told himself. If they weren't real, then none of them—neither his father nor mother nor Jena—might be real either.

His father looked out the window. A dark band the color of iodine rimmed the far end of the lake. "Looks like rain," he said.

"But there's not much left to do, is there?" Frank said.

"Oh, there's a lot to do. We've got to mow the lawn, clean the chimney—"

"You mean cap it, don't you?"

"No, I mean *clean* it. That's something you can do. I don't like going up on the ladder anymore. I don't like heights."

"Dad, you don't need to clean the chimney. Let the new people worry about it."

"It hasn't been cleaned in two years."

"But it just isn't *necessary.*"

His father shook his head. "It should be done."

"Dad, it's a waste of time!"

"Why are you in such a hurry, Frank? Where are you going anyway?"

"Well, if you think it's so important," Frank snapped, "you do it."

His father worked his lips the way he did when he was upset, then walked out of the bedroom and down the stairs. The porch door slammed.

Frank slapped his palm against the wall. *It's happening again,* he thought, *the arguing.* It was nothing they could escape. He paced the room, glanced out the window, sat on the bed. He heard a creaking noise. He rose and looked out the window again. His father went by pushing a splayed wheelbarrow containing bricks, rags, and a burlap bag—materials to make a cleaning bag for the chimney. Frank pulled a chair up to the window and watched. His father dumped the wheelbarrow's contents onto the ground, then disappeared around the side of the house. In a few minutes he was back, a ladder precariously balanced on his shoulder.

Frank went downstairs and leaned against the porch railing. His father was stuffing the burlap bag with rags and bricks.

"How are you going to carry that up the ladder?" Frank asked.

His father didn't reply.

"Dad, look. Do you want me to do it?"

His father nodded toward the hose under the kitchen window. "You didn't put that away."

"You'll need it to soak the cleaning bag," Frank retorted. "Won't you?"

His father looped clothesline around the neck of the bag and jerked it tight. "Did you turn off the water heater?"

Frank slapped his hand against his thigh. "I knew you'd ask that! I just knew it. Yes, I turned off the goddam water heater."

His father dragged the heavy bag to the foot of the ladder. Grasping a side rail with one hand and holding the bag with the other, he mounted unsteadily.

He'll break his neck, Frank thought.

His father climbed another few rungs, clutching the ladder tightly, leaning into it for support.

Frank went down the porch steps. "Dad, come on down. I'll do it."

"No!"

Frank went to the foot of the ladder and grasped the bottom of the bag. Above him, his father yanked, but Frank held on. "Dad, let's not argue anymore, okay? I said I'd do it."

"You don't want to."

"I don't want you to break your neck! Please. Just come on down."

"I can *do* it," his father said, but didn't move. Frank tugged again, and now his father did climb down. He dropped the bag at the foot of the ladder. "I'll go mow the lawn," he said, not looking at Frank.

When he was out of sight, Frank kicked the bag, hard. Then he readjusted the ladder, slung the heavy bag over his shoulder, and climbed. He pushed it onto the roof and went down for the hose. The cardinal had returned, still hopping about it. "Beat it," Frank barked. On the other side of the house, the lawn mower sputtered and came to life. Frank coupled the hose to the outside spigot and hauled it up the ladder.

He wet the burlap bag and lowered it down the chimney. When it touched bottom, Frank raised it, then lowered it again, over and over. His arms ached from the bag's weight. When he withdrew it, the bag was black with ash. *Maybe some of this is from the fire Jena and I made years ago,* he thought. After all, it could be: his parents—and any renters—had probably been here only in spring and summer. He rubbed his fingers in the ash, then rubbed some on his arm, his cheek.

Crazy, he thought. He wet his hands with hose water and

washed his arms and face. He hosed down the bag. Sooty water ran down the roof. He stomped on the bag to squeeze out more.

His father went by below, more pulled by the lawn mower than pushing it. He'd taken off his chinos and put on old plaid Bermuda shorts with a tear that ran from pocket to leg. His belt slipped from the flesh of his waist, and his thin legs were white, almost hairless now. His jaw was thrust forward, intent on the grass before him.

He's gotten frailer, Frank thought. A tenderness, warm and unbidden, almost made Frank call—to say what, he didn't know. The mower spluttered, coughed, and died. His father knelt down and extracted a thick clump of earth and grass. He turned it over in his fingers, as if it were something rare and marvelous, then tossed it away. He restarted the mower and was gone.

Although the sun was bright and warm above, the southern sky was now storm-dark. Frank descended, found the chimney cap in the cellar, climbed up again, and covered the chimney. With a grunt, he heaved the bag off the roof. He climbed back down, started to untie the bag, then hesitated. His father would never need this again. Frank waited until the lawn mower was on the far side of the house, then dragged the bag to the edge of the dock and dropped it into the lake. It splashed thickly and sank. Ripples slapped the pilings; the rope swing swayed gently in the breeze. Frank stood, hands on hips, and stared at it.

He imagined a young boy high in the tree, hands tensed around the rope, his flesh shivery with fear and anticipation. The ever-so-far-away water's shifts and shimmerings made the boy dizzy. He would never, could never jump . . . it was too far, too high, his parents were right . . . and then he *would* be falling, plunging into the water's chill, swallowed by darkness. And then up again, breaking the surface, restored to a world of sunlight and life. Frank envied that boy. How brave he was! He was afraid, yet he jumped. He fell, and fell free.

That was me, he thought. He had been that boy.

Frank walked up to the house. His father had finished cutting the grass. "Well, this is mine," he said. He pushed the mower to the car and put it in the trunk. "The new people don't get it." He looked at Frank. "You don't need a mower, do you?"

"Not for an apartment, Dad."

"No, I guess not. Well, all done?"

"Yep."

"Put the bag away?"

Frank nodded.

"Well, we're getting to the end now. We can do the storm shutters and drain the pipes after lunch."

"Maybe we should just keep going, Dad," Frank suggested. "It's going to rain."

"We've got time. Let's eat."

His father got the cooler from the back seat. They sat on the porch steps and ate a lunch of tuna-fish sandwiches, macaroni salad, sweet pickles, and grapes. Frank opened beers and handed one to his father. The light had turned leaden, and the clouds which had been massing at the far end of the lake now rolled overhead, imparting a dull sheen to the water. The breeze curled their paper napkins. Frank flicked a ladybug from his knee. He looked at his father. The older man seemed lost in thought, raising sandwich to mouth in slow, careful movements, almost unaware that he was eating. Frank leaned back against the steps and breathed deeply. The lake smelled old and moldering, like the underside of a decaying log.

"So, how are you doing?" his father asked.

"Fine. I'm getting along."

"Is it okay? Where you're living?"

"It's small. An efficiency." Frank laughed. "It's not much bigger than my old room here."

"Ah."

"It suits me," Frank said.

They lapsed again into silence. Frank folded his napkin, opened it, folded it again. His father cleared his throat. "I just don't know why you never came back."

"What do you mean, Dad?"

His father waved to indicate the lake, the house. "All these years, you never came back here. Right after college—bingo! You were gone. Off to Greece, to California. Wherever you are now. You could've spent a few weeks here in the summer with your mother and me. But you never did."

"Dad, you know how things are—"

"No." His father looked at him sharply. "How are they?"

"I married Jena. We moved to another state—"

"You could've brought Jena here. We kept inviting the two of you. You know how much we liked her."

"We came at Christmas—"

"No—*here*. In summer."

Frank pursed his lips.

"We could've all been together in the summer," his father said. "It would've made your mother happy."

"Dad, don't make me feel bad about this." Frank began clearing the remnants of their lunch. "There's just no need to." He tossed the plastic utensils and paper plates into a grocery bag.

"How is Jena?" his father asked.

"Fine." Frank snapped the lids onto the salad containers. "She's fine."

"Still in California?"

"As far as I know."

"What's she doing now?"

"I really don't know."

"Don't you talk to her?"

"Dad"—Frank held out his hands, palms up, as if in supplication—"we're divorced. She lives in another state."

"Everybody seems to live in another state," his father murmured.

"It's over with us, Dad. Dead and buried."

"That's what happens with the woman you loved? You declare her dead? You just bury her?"

"Let's not talk about this anymore, okay?" Frank walked to the trash barrel and threw the garbage bag in.

"Don't leave it there," his father called. "There won't be another pickup till spring."

"Jesus!" Frank retrieved the bag, opened the car door, and hurled it into the footwell. He got inside and closed the door. Thunder rumbled. He rolled up the window. And remembered: when he'd been here before, with his mother, it had rained, too. Did everything, all the time, repeat itself? Was the past like a hawk, endlessly circling, ready at any time to plummet and strike?

Frank got out. His father was staring at the lake and didn't look at him when he came up.

"I want to ask you something," Frank said. "You blame me for not giving you any grandchildren, don't you?"

His father looked at him. "It's not my business."

"But you do, don't you?"

His father rose. "I'm going to get the storm shutters."

"Well, I'm *glad* we didn't have kids. I mean, look what happened."

"I don't know why you say that like you're proud," his father snapped.

"You know it was me who didn't want kids, don't you? She told you, didn't she?"

His father stared at him, surprised. "What do you mean?"

"She told me about visiting you, Dad. About staying there . . ."

His father worked his lips, then strode across the lawn to the cellar. Frank followed. They descended into its musty light and coolness.

"You think it's my fault that Jena and me split, don't you?"

His father pulled the canvas off the storm shutters.

"You do, don't you?"

"What does it matter?" his father said. "You've never cared what I think anyway."

"You know, she's not so spotless, your darling Jena. I could tell you stories about her. Or maybe you know that, too."

His father blinked. "What are you talking about?"

"She told me how . . . you hugged and everything . . ."

His father looked stunned. He opened his mouth as if to say something, then lifted a shutter and brushed by Frank.

"Did you want to sleep with her?" Frank called. "Did you?" As soon as he said it, he was ashamed. He heard his father drop the shutter on the ground and walk back to the cellar. The older man pulled and tugged to free another shutter. Numbly, Frank helped. They worked together in tense silence until all of the shutters were piled outside. The sky was much darker, and a small chop had picked up on the lake. Frank could smell the rain, ripe and hushed.

"Dad," Frank said. "Look, I'm sorry—"

"I did want to sleep with her." His father lifted a shutter and rested it on his knee. "I don't know why we didn't."

Frank's heart, his throat, his very soul ached. Mechanically, he carried a shutter to a window and hooked it over the frame. It didn't fit precisely—the wood had warped—so he had to jam it in place. His father still stood by the pile of shutters, arms crossed, head slightly bowed. Frank walked back and lifted another shutter.

"Do you want to know why I never came back?" Frank's voice was quavering. "Do you really want to know? Because I couldn't *wait* to get away from you. Do you understand? I just couldn't *wait* to get away!" He let the shutter clatter and fall. "I still can't."

His father blinked, then turned and walked down the slope toward the lake.

Frank picked up the shutter and carried it to the window. He slapped it in place, then slapped it again and again, till his palm ached. The first droplets of rain spattered the ground. He went back to the pile and saw his father on the dock, arms folded, gazing over the water. *I won't feel guilty,* Frank thought. *Not this time, no.* Yet when he picked up another shutter, he hesitated. "Dad!" he yelled. "It's raining." His father didn't seem to hear.

"We've got to finish this," he called. But his father didn't move.

All right, Frank thought, *stand there. I'll take care of it myself.*

Hurrying to beat the downpour, Frank finished putting the storm shutters on the lower-floor windows. He imagined the interior of the house becoming progressively darker as the shutters cut off the last light that could seep inside. *Like it's going to bed,* his mother used to tell him as a child, *going to sleep for the winter, and when spring comes, we'll wake it up.* Well, no more. Everything was asleep for good. No one would wake it now.

A bolt of lightning crackled over the lake. Rain began falling harder, in thick, scattered drops. Frank's arms ached, and he still had the upper windows to do. He returned to the back and looked at the dock. He couldn't see his father. "Dad?" he called. The breeze gusting off the lake made him shiver. Frank walked to the water's edge. He scanned the cove. "Dad! Where are you?"

He heard a rustling in the trees that overarched the water, and looked up. His father stood high above on the limb by the rope swing. He was breathing heavily from the climb.

"Dad, what the hell are you doing up there!"

"How . . . high . . ." his father panted.

"What?"

"I wanted to see . . . how high this really was."

"What are you talking about?"

"You said it wasn't that high." His father held tight to the rope on the slippery limb. "I wanted to see."

"So now you've seen. Come on down before you break your neck!"

"You're right," he said. "It's not that high."

"Dad, what does it matter? Just get on down."

His father tugged on the rope. "You know, it wasn't your mother who didn't want you to swing from here. It was me." Rain pattered on the leaves, and the branches creaked in the gathering wind. "I don't know what I was afraid of."

"Dad—"

His father waved as if saluting, then grasped the thick rope with both hands and swung out over the cove, his shirt fluttering behind. Frank opened his mouth, but no sound came out, the only cry his father's as he reached the far point of his arc and let go, the rope falling away as he fell, arms swinging, into the lake. He landed bent over, partly on his stomach. The water churned where he'd entered.

"Dad," Frank murmured in disbelief.

He waited for his father to come up. But he didn't. Nothing moved on the water except the pocking of rain and the fast-receding ripples from his father's plunge.

"Dad?" Frank called. He went onto the dock and peered into the rain-flecked water. The lake was dark; he could see nothing below. Lightning stitched the sky.

"Dad!" he screamed. "Oh Jesus—" Frank ran to the dock's edge. He tore off one shoe and had the other in his hand when his father surfaced with a whoop farther down the cove. He shook his head like a playful seal and began to breaststroke slowly toward him. Frank sat down, his legs dangling like a helpless marionette's over the edge of the dock. He seemed to be laughing and crying at the same time, and try as he might, he couldn't stop. His father must have been confused, since he cried out, "What's the matter?" and "What's wrong?" but Frank could only shake his head, and raise his hand, and let it drop.

"I thought you were dead," he said, the words choked, as if it were he who had been drowning. He dropped the other shoe into the water and held out his now-empty hands. "I thought you were dead, but you weren't."

Part IV

HOMECOMING

Homecoming

—Summer 1987

I *was back in* Southern California on business last week, and on an impulse drove through the town where Jena and I used to live. I turned down our street and went by our old house. Amazingly, a For Sale sign was staked on the lawn, just as it had been on closing day six years ago, when the couple who'd bought it from us had taken possession. I drove slowly by, then doubled back. No car was in the drive. I stopped and contemplated the house. They'd repainted it a dull, lemony color, which I wasn't sure I liked. *The first thing we'll do, of course, is repaint,* the husband had said on closing day. *Then we'll redo the floors.* He spoke as if he were a surgeon with a tricky case. I'd disliked both of them immensely. He seemed so cocksure, while his wife, a mousy woman with bad teeth, nodded at everything he said. *Well, you just live here awhile,* I thought. Jena and I had had a bad argument the day before while clearing out some last things, so I was feeling sad and irritable and uncomfortable anyway. Then we all shook hands—the real estate agent, the buyers, Jena and I—and soon the agent left, and the couple walked inside, and Jena and I were left standing there, feeling strange. And that was it, finis, good-bye to the house. Jena moved to Redondo Beach, and I went back to Michigan and then, just last year, to Pittsburgh, to be closer to my father, who'd had a heart attack. I hadn't seen the house, or Jena, since.

I got out of the car and walked to the door. I wanted to see what else these people had done with the house; I wanted to see *how* they'd done with it. I tried to remember their name, but couldn't: like so much from the early days of my divorce, I'd blanked it out. I rang the bell. Nobody came. I rang again, waited, then walked down the steps and looked through a window into the living room that used to be mine. It was empty. They'd already moved out. I went around back to the patio. The live-oak tree that shaded the house had been trimmed back. Ornamental vines now entwined a new wrought-iron fence, and geraniums grew in a boxed terrace. I peered into the back bedroom where I'd seen Jena dancing by herself six years before. The wallpaper had been taken off, and the walls repainted.

I had to admit, it looked as if these people had taken pretty good care of the place. They'd done things, made improvements, something Jena and I never seemed able to do. Somehow we never could agree on what to do with the house, and so nothing got done. She always wanted to fix, improve, decorate; I didn't. If she'd had her way, we'd have constantly been retiling, regrouting, repaneling. That was stuff my father would be interested in, not me, I told her. To me a house was just to live in. There were more important things to spend money on. Greece, for example. I'd started fantasizing about going back to Greece again, which later, disastrously, we did.

"We don't live in Greece," Jena said. "We live here."

After walking all the way around the house, I got back in my car and sat thinking. It was hard to understand now why I cared, why she cared, to argue so intensely about the house. *Just wood, paint, plaster,* I thought. *Things.* I felt sad and guilty, as if the house were a person I'd failed.

"It's a nice house," I said aloud.

And then I remembered the keys.

I'd always kept a spare set under a flagstone on the patio. Maybe they were still there. I felt my cheeks flush as I walked around back. How many flagstones from the corner was it? Five? Six? I turned over the fifth flagstone. Nothing—and nothing was under the sixth one, either. Maybe I remembered wrong, or the owners had found them. But how could they? I never told them about the keys. At the closing I'd meant to show them my hiding place and save them the trouble of making a spare set. But everything was happening so fast, I forgot. We'd all shaken hands and signed checks and documents and inspection reports, they took the keys we gave them, we shook hands again, they walked into our house, and everything was settled. It wasn't until later that I remembered I hadn't told them about the other keys.

Settled, I thought. And suddenly I knew where those keys were. I turned over the fifth flagstone again, dug into the moist earth, and, about an inch below the surface, I found them, slightly tarnished, still on their plastic ring. I went back to the front door, hoping they hadn't changed the locks. I inserted the key into the bottom lock for the first time in six years. It turned. I unlocked the top one, and pushed open the door. If anyone wondered what I was doing, I'd tell them I came to look at the house, that I was a friend of the owner and he'd given me the keys. I wasn't breaking and entering. And I wasn't trying to hide anything: there was my car in the drive.

Early evening light spilled onto the hardwood floor.

They'd resanded and repolished, just as they'd said. It did look better, I'd grant them that. In the kitchen, they'd laid down blue-and-white terra-cotta tiling, installed oak cupboards, and— biggest change of all—built a butcher-block work station in the center, complete with sink, sliding drawers, and racks. Jena had always wanted one. Well, here it was. *I should take a picture and send it to her,* I thought. I flicked on the lights: they worked. I turned on the stove. The gas sputtered, lit. Why had they left the utilities on? And then I realized: the real estate agent would have to demonstrate that everything worked when she took buyers through. I picked up the phone. The line hummed. This really surprised me. Why had they left it connected? Had they *just* left? I glanced back into the living room, as if they might come in any moment. Well, if they did, I'd explain about the keys, my curiosity. It would be all right. After all, what was left here to steal?

I wandered from room to room. They'd all been repainted and the carpeting removed. Wall-length mirrors and a new tub had been put in the master bath, and they'd installed a cedar railing on the sundeck. In the guest bedroom, I saw a possible reason for the phone being connected: someone was painting in there. Brushes were carefully laid out on the ladder, and paint cans were lined up on a dropcloth. They must have left a line connected for the workmen. Or maybe they were doing it them- selves. *These people never stop,* I thought. *Six years later, they're still working on the house.*

Back in the living room, I noticed speaker grilles built into the wall. Underneath the grilles was a cabinet door. I opened it and found a built-in receiver and tape deck. I turned it on. Music from an easy-listening station filled the room. I remembered seeing those same speaker grilles in the master bedroom. I walked back there, and all along the hall I heard music. It came from all the rooms. They'd wired the entire house for sound. Incredible. I went back to the living room and turned the music off. I shook my head in admiration. I had to admit it: they'd really done things right.

I went out to the patio. It was cooling off rapidly, the way it does in the evening in Southern California. I thought how funny it all was: much of the time we lived here I'd wanted to be free of the house, and then I was, yet here I was back again. I breathed deeply and smelled sage drifting down from the foothills. *The ivy needs watering,* I thought. I turned on the sprinklers, and they whirled and twirled merrily. I wondered if Antonio still took care of things. *Herrera,* I thought. Antonio Herrera. I was proud of myself for remembering his name.

That's what I can say, I thought, *if anybody asks what I'm doing here.* I could say I was taking care of things. I sat on the patio steps and listened to the sound of water on bush and stone and ivy. And I had a wonderful idea: Why stay at a motel tonight? Why not just spend the night here? I could park my car along the street. When it got dark, I'd turn off all the lights so I wouldn't be seen. The thought of staying in our old house, in our old bedroom, gave me a delightful shiver. Besides, it was satisfying to think that I—not those other people—would sleep here last.

I turned off the sprinklers, phoned the motel in Los Angeles, and canceled my reservation. Then I drove to the shopping center down Foothill Boulevard. At the drugstore I bought an air mattress and a newspaper. And I had another great idea. I bought one of those cheap Polaroid cameras and some film packs: I'd take pictures of rooms in the house and send them to Jena. She could see all the changes they'd made. On the way back, I bought a six-pack, then stopped at Burger Chef for some cheeseburgers and onion rings. I was celebrating, after all: I'd come back home.

It was dusk when I returned. I turned the sprinklers back

on. Then I put the beer in the refrigerator, spread a section of the paper on the floor as a tablecloth, and sat down cross-legged to eat. I decided to chance keeping the lights on for a while. After all, I could be an agent showing the house. Or the owners—I could be them. Through the window I watched the evening deepen until all the blue-green had seeped out of the sky, and there was nothing left but night. I ate, and drank my beer, and listened to the water on the ivy, sounding just like rain, just as it did when we lived here.

And somehow, try as I might, I couldn't figure it out: how I'd come to be sitting here now, alone in an empty house. The memories were all there—the years, the events—but somehow I couldn't make the connections. It had the no-logic of a dream, a crumble-jumble of scene shifts and changing faces. It was like nodding off in the movies, something I used to do all the time, and waking up disoriented, not knowing what had happened in the picture. *What's happened?* I'd ask Jena, and she'd whisper, *I can't explain now.* I had to figure out what I missed as best I could. Now I'd awakened to find the house empty, and Jena gone. It had all happened in my sleep somehow, without my ever knowing or intending it.

I crumpled my beer can and tossed it into the trash bag. *You have to stay awake,* I thought. *Or you might miss something.*

I loaded the camera and went through the house taking pictures. I couldn't get all of a room in the frame, so I had to take a lot of pictures from different angles. Sometimes I just photographed details, like the kitchen work-station, or the built-in speakers. I wondered if Jena would even recognize some of the rooms. In the Polaroids, with the color off and the lighting bad, some of them didn't look like the real rooms at all. I didn't know whether she could tell how nicely they'd fixed things up. After photographing each room, I turned off the light, and when I was done, the house was dark.

I got another beer from the kitchen. I hesitated, then unplugged the phone from its jack, went back to the bedroom, and plugged it into the jack there. I looked up Jena's number in my address book and called her. Not more than forty miles away, her phone rang.

She answered on the third ring, her voice thicker, darker than I remembered, and for a moment I just couldn't speak.

"Hello?" she said again.

"It's me," I said. That's all I could say.

"Frank? Frank, is that you?"

"It's me," I repeated dumbly. It felt like a thick sludge coated my throat.

"Well . . . I—just a minute," she said. "I've got to turn something off."

She sounded flustered. I cleared my throat a few times, and felt the muscles loosen. Was she really gone? "Jena?" I said. "Jena?"

She picked up the phone again. "What a surprise," she said. "How are you?"

"I'm fine, Jena. How're you?"

"Fine. Just fine."

"How's . . . Peter, right?" She'd married again, I knew. I'd heard it from Jillian, that old friend of ours who, no matter where I moved, faithfully kept in touch.

"He's fine. Frank, why are you calling? Where are you?"

"In the area."

"Here? In Los Angeles?"

"Just passing through. I thought I'd say hello. We haven't talked in a long time, Jena."

"No. Well. What a surprise." Her voice was sounding more like I remembered it now—brighter, younger. It was Jena again. My wife. "How's your father?" she asked.

"Fine. He's fine. No—actually he's been a little sick, Jena. He had a small heart attack."

"Oh God! When?"

"Last year. But he's okay. He's recovering well."

"I didn't even know! You should have told me, Frank. I would've sent a card or something."

"You still can, Jena. He'd like that."

"Well, maybe I will."

"I've moved again, you know. I'm not in Michigan anymore. I'm in Pittsburgh."

"My God." She laughed. "I thought you *hated* Pennsylvania."

"I wanted to be a little closer to Dad. He's getting older, Jena."

"Jesus, we all are."

"He's just not been the same since Mom died. You know. And then this heart attack really scared him."

"He always was a little sad." Jena said. "His outlook, I mean."

We were quiet for a moment.

"Well, I'll write him," Jena said. "I really will."

"He'd like that, Jena."

"Give him my best, Frank."

"I will. I . . . I know he'd send his love." And then I said something strange: "Maybe he should've married you, Jena. I mean, ideally. In the best of all possible worlds. Where ages match up and people find each other and everything." I was kidding, but then realized I was half-serious too.

Jena laughed. "I did the next best thing, didn't I? I married you." Then she was silent. For a moment I thought she wasn't there anymore.

"Jena?" I said.

"Um-hmmm?"

"Guess where I am now. You'll never guess where."

"I don't know, Frank. Where?"

"Where is the last place in the world you'd think I'd be calling from?"

"Frank, I've got no idea."

"Our old house," I said triumphantly.

"What?"

"Our old house. The one you and I lived in."

"On Gilmour Street?"

"Hey—what other house did we ever live in?"

"What are you doing there, Frank? Who's there now? Those people we sold it to?"

"Nope. I'm here by myself." I explained to her about driving by, seeing the house for sale, finding my old set of keys.

"My God, you just went *in?*"

"Yep. I'm in our old bedroom right now."

"Jesus, Frank. I can't believe it."

"I'm going to stay here tonight, too."

"What do you mean you're *staying* there?"

"I'm going to sleep on the floor. I've got an air mattress."

"Frank, are you serious?" She said this with a little disbelieving laugh.

"Hey—I've got a newspaper. I'm drinking beer. I've got everything I need."

"Frank, you're crazy. You'll get *arrested.* "

"Nobody will see me. I've got all the lights off now. I'm talking to you in the dark."

"My God, you're breaking and entering!"

"Entering. Not breaking. Besides, this was my house."

"*Was*, Frank. Was."

"I used my own key to—"

"It's still illegal, Frank."

"You know what I mean. I could explain."

"Frank, it is *still*—"

"The place looks good, Jena. They've done nice things to it."

"I just can't *believe* this—"

"You ought to come over," I said. "You're only forty miles away, right?"

A pause. And then she laughed. "You must've gotten a lot crazier since I knew you, Frank."

"I am. I'm a lot crazier, Jena." My voice caught. "I'm different."

"How? Tell me."

"Well—I'm here. I do crazy things."

"Like what? What else?"

I couldn't think what else. Instead I said, "Wouldn't that be something, Jena? If you came over? You and me back here?"

"I'd have a hard time explaining it to Peter."

"He's that lawyer you told me about, right?"

"What? When?"

"The last day here. When we were cleaning the last stuff out of the house, remember? You told me a story about a lawyer who got a strange phone call from a guy whose wife was dying—"

"My God, Frank. You're right! How do you *remember* that?"

"Is Peter there now?"

"No. He's at a meeting."

"Well, you can do it then. Come over, I mean."

"Oh sure." She laughed again. "What do you look like now, Frank?"

"I'm taller. Handsomer."

"My, my."

"I've got some distinguished gray." That was so—along with less hair, too. My hairline was receding as my waist was thickening. Nothing serious in either area yet, but I could see it all coming. My body wasn't going to give me a free ride anymore, that was for sure. "Why don't you come over and see?" I said.

"Frank, I don't think so."

"Come on. Where's your sense of adventure?" I tried to say it lightly. "You always said we needed more adventure in our lives, Jena. Here's your chance."

"That was then, Frank."

"And now you don't? Have adventures, I mean?"

She was silent a moment. "You were my adventure, Frank. I just didn't know it."

I didn't say anything.

"It was enough," she said.

I have to say something, I thought. If the silence became too long, I might never be able to speak again. "So—how're things with you and Peter?"

"I told you. Fine."

"You don't sound too enthusiastic."

"Don't read things into this, Frank." Her voice seemed to tighten. "Things are fine."

"Hey—I'm glad, Jena."

A pause. "We've been trying to have a baby," she said. "Oh?"

"No luck so far, but we're trying."

"Well, I hope you do, Jena," I said. "I know how much you wanted that. You . . . you deserve it." I felt regret on my tongue, like a bitter herb. "You know, sometimes I think we should've had kids."

She laughed. "We were the kids, Frank."

Another pause, which became another silence.

"You're really there alone?" she asked.

"Yep. It's completely empty. Except for some painting they're doing in the guest bedroom. They're *still* fixing things up, Jena. They're like beavers."

She was quiet again, as if she were thinking about that. Outside, I could hear the cicadas, and the sprinklers sounding like rain.

"Do you hear the cicadas?" I asked. "Listen." I held the phone away.

"I . . . think so."

"Just like Greece, remember?" And then, thinking maybe I shouldn't have said that, too many bad memories, I said, "I'm watering out back. Can you hear it?" I held the phone away again.

"I don't know," she said.

"It looked a little dry, so I've been watering."

"You're amazing, Frank." She sounded impressed.

"I may even do a little of their painting for them. Help a little." I don't know why I said this. The thought never even occurred to me until that moment.

"Frank, I'd leave that alone, if I were you."

"Why? Don't you think I can paint?"

"No. I mean, it's none of your business. Don't mess with things that aren't yours."

"They've done nice things to the kitchen here, Jena," I said. "They've put a cooking island in the middle."

"Really? That's exactly what I wanted to do, remember?"

"Well, they did it."

"What's it made out of?"

"Some kind of white wood. It smells good. It's got a sink and a butcher-block counter."

"You never wanted to put one in."

"It does look nice," I admitted.

"So they did it," she murmured. And then was silent again.

"Jena? You there?"

"Tell me what else they did, Frank." Her voice was low, as if she were standing right next to me.

"Well, they—" I remembered the sound system. "Wait, Jena. Hold on." I ran into the living room and turned on the receiver. I found a station playing soft jazz, ran back, and turned up the volume control in the bedroom. "Listen." I held the phone away. "Can you hear that?"

"Music?"

"They've got the whole house wired for sound, Jena. Isn't that wonderful? You can hear it everywhere. Every damn room."

"Amazing," she said. I could tell she was impressed.

"Now I'll tell you all about the house," I said. "You just sit back." With the music as background, I lowered my voice, as if only the smallest of distances separated us now and I could whisper in her ear, smell the warmth of her skin, the fragrance of her hair. I told her about everything. I gave her the tour of the house, room by room. I wanted to tell it to her so well she could see it. And when I was finished, she said, "It sounds nice," and then she was quiet.

"You ought to come over," I said. "Jena?" I heard these small sounds, little gasps almost, as if she were having trouble breathing. "Jena, what's wrong?" And as soon as I said it, I knew she was crying, and trying not to. "Honey? What's the matter? What's wrong?"

"You son of a bitch."

I was startled. "Why did you say that? What did I do?"

"Frank, you get out of there. Get out of there right now!"

"But I . . . what—"

"I want you out of there right now. You've got no *business* being there."

"Jena—"

"You're a housebreaker! That house is *not* yours."

"Jena, why are you—"

"You don't belong there!"

"You *can't* tell me to get out," I said. "It's not your house either."

"I'm going to call those people and tell them you're there—"

"You can't! You don't remember their name either."

"Then I'll call the police!"

"You do that, Jena. Just go ahead! I'll stay right here."

"You think I'm kidding, Frank. You—"

"You just couldn't leave this alone, could you? Everything was nice, I was telling you about the house, and then you had to spoil things."

"You called me!" she cried. "You called me!" Her voice broke, and she was crying again. I was afraid she'd hang up, but she didn't. "All I wanted was a nice house," she said, sniffling. "My God, so little—"

"It *is* a nice house, Jena." I waited for her to say something, but she didn't. "It can be fixed," I said.

"No," she said. "I don't live there anymore."

And now I was silent.

"Go home, Frank." She sounded tired. "Turn off the music, lock up, go home. I won't call the police. Just go home."

"I'm staying," I said.

She hung up then, after all. I listened, as if somehow, magically, she might come back, and then I hung up too. I turned off the music and the sprinklers. The house was silent. I lay down on my air mattress, finished my beer, and thought

a long while, although later I couldn't remember anything I'd
been thinking—it was all just drifting images, like garbage on
the sea. I went to the guest bedroom and turned on the light.
I opened a paint can, hefted the brushes. I held one over the
paint and hesitated, then put it back on the rung of the ladder
and closed the can. Even though I hadn't done anything, my
hands smelled of paint. I washed them, and washed them. Then
I went back and sat down again on the mattress. I shuffled
through the Polaroids of the rooms, trying to see them in what
little light remained. I'd forgotten to tell Jena about them. The
night seemed to draw closer, as if it were staring at me. I thought
of calling her back, but then didn't.

   There wasn't much you could do by yourself in an empty
house at night. I took a shower in the dark, brushed my teeth,
and, still naked, lay down to sleep. I set my travel alarm for five:
I'd be out before anybody came by in the morning.

   Sometime during the night—I don't know whether it was
hours or only minutes later—I woke. The phone was ringing and
ringing. I couldn't move, and I was afraid that whoever was
calling would hang up before I could get to it. With a mighty
effort, I rose and was walking toward the kitchen before I realized the phone wasn't there, it was by my mattress, and it hadn't
been ringing at all.

   "A dream," I murmured.

   I saw a light in the living room. "Jena?" I called. But no
one was there. And then I remembered I'd turned on the light
when I shut off the sound system, and must have forgotten to
turn it off. Why the police hadn't stopped to see what was going
on in a supposedly empty house, I have no idea. Even then, if
anybody had been looking through the curtainless windows, they
would have seen a man, naked as the night, walking hesitantly
through the room. Back in the bedroom, I sat in the dark. I

didn't want to know what time it was: it was enough that it was dark.

I put on jogging shorts and a T-shirt, and put the clock and my shaving kit into my suitcase. I stuffed in the trash bag from dinner. I threw the Polaroids in—maybe I'd mail them later to Jena. Finally, I unplugged the phone and tossed it in, too. I put the suitcase in my car and started the engine. Then I went back into the house and went from room to room, hurriedly, like a thief. I turned on the lights in the living room, the kitchen, the master bedroom, the guest bedroom, the patio; I turned on every light in the house and every light outside the house. It looked great, as if a lot of people were expected. I turned on the sound system so that music played in all the rooms. Then I turned on the sprinklers. All around the house, water was falling. I opened up every door—front door, kitchen door, hall door, patio. I opened the garage doors, and I even opened the door to the utility shed. I let the night come in. I stood by the car for a minute to look at it all, to see what I'd done.

See what you missed. The thought ran through my head. Maybe that's what I'd write on the note I'd enclose with the Polaroids: SEE WHAT YOU MISSED. I'd send them to her. Or maybe I'd just keep them myself. After all, they were mine.

See what you missed . . .

At least one of us should read that, I thought. At least one of us should understand.

Stand

—July 1988

Some things you just couldn't seem to say good-bye to, Frank thought as he drove up the dirt road to the summer house. His father had sold it five years ago after his mother died, and Frank hadn't been back since helping him close it for the last time. Now his father was dead too, these last six months, not of the second heart attack he'd feared so much, but suddenly, of a stroke. At age forty-four—mother and father dead, Jena gone, no children—Frank was alone. Sometimes he felt this aloneness as the freedom he'd always imagined he desired. He could go anywhere, do anything, and as if to prove this to himself, he bought an old Triumph TR-3 and began driving on weekends into the Pennsylvania countryside. These trips had no real desti-nation and usually ended with his drinking beer in some overly air-conditioned motel lounge, then driving back to Pittsburgh with the radio tuned full blast to an oldies station. Now, on this Fourth of July weekend, he had come back up here, near the New York border, to the summer house by the lake.

The new owners, whoever they were, were gone—strange, since it was the holiday weekend. The door was locked, the deck chairs neatly stacked. Frank peered through the porch window, but the sun's slant was wrong, and he could see nothing. He walked down to the dock and looked at the rope swing still hanging over the water. Frank felt his knees ache—one already had a touch of arthritis—just from thinking about the climb up to the rope. What separated the boy of then, his skin pimply as a chicken's in anticipation of the lake's coldness, from the middle-aged man of now? What country had he passed through if not that of Time, which, like a desert of swirling sand, had erased itself behind him? Everything had happened to him there, and yet somehow, he felt, nothing had. Frank looked up at the house. Everyone he thought he'd loved had been here with him, and all were gone. He should be, too.

He was alone, he told himself, but he was free.

Still . . . the early evening was fine and musky, and Frank had no desire to return yet to Pittsburgh. He'd seen posters at a gas station announcing a fireworks display at the lake. He glanced at his watch: only a few hours till the show. He could drive back to Pittsburgh afterwards, or get a motel room along the way. Frank drove down the road to the Mini-Mart and bought chicken-salad sandwiches, potato chips, and a six-pack. On a display rack, he saw a Yankees baseball cap much like one he'd had as a boy. He bought that, too.

The beach was crowded with swimmers and barbecuers and volleyballers. Frank wanted to be more alone. A quarter-mile past the beach, the asphalt turned into a narrow dirt road that threaded through thick pines which hid the shore. Frank was about to back up when he came upon an unexpected clearing with picnic tables and a dock that jutted into the lake. He heard voices and smelled charcoal. Two pickups, a Ford and a Chevy, were parked off the road. He pulled up beside them: at least it would be quieter here than down at the beach. From the dock he should have a good view of the fireworks.

Four men shared the clearing with him. One was turning hamburgers and hot dogs on a hugely smoking grill while his friend solemnly watched. The other two lazily passed a football, catching with one hand while holding beers with the other. Except for one of the football throwers, who was clean-shaven and long-haired and seemed younger than the rest, they were all bearded and T-shirted in a slouched country way. Local boys, Frank thought. He took a beer from his six-pack and walked down to the dock to sit apart from them. The grill-tender nodded as Frank passed, and his friend belched. The football players ignored him.

Frank sat on the dock and drank his beer. The lowering sun scattered thin rays through the trees on the opposite shore. He shaded his eyes and searched for the summer house, but couldn't find it. He raised his beer in a farewell salute and felt strangely guilty, as if he were abandoning the house, leaving it to chance and ruin. *It's not mine at all,* he reminded himself. It was nothing he had to care for.

A breeze raked the water. Frank crushed his beer can and walked back to the car for the sandwiches. The two men who'd been throwing the football were inspecting the Triumph. The heavyset one had a puffy, bearded face that seemed not to have settled right that day. He nodded to Frank while his friend, the clean-shaven one, grinned. Up close he wasn't as young as he'd seemed—the long hair had contributed to that illusion. He was, if anything, Frank's age. The corners of his eyes were crinkled, as if he'd been squinting at something for a long time.

"Nice car." He rubbed his thumb along the fender, so that it squeaked.

"Thanks," Frank said.

"You sure don't see too many of these. Old Porsches, MG's, you see a lot of. Not these."

"I've noticed that," Frank said. He opened the car door and took out the sandwich bag. He had no real desire to talk.

"Ride nice?"

"It's okay."

"I always wanted to have one of these, didn't you, Polk?" His friend grunted. "It's really something." He patted the Triumph's fender. "Course, I'd never give up my little beauty." He nodded toward the Ford pickup. "You need a truck around here more'n a sports car."

"Where you from?" the other man asked Frank. His voice was thick and tarry.

"Pittsburgh."

"What brings you up here?"

"The fireworks," Frank said lightly.

"Shit, man. You come all the way here for fireworks? Don't they got fireworks in Pittsburgh?"

"I was visiting," Frank said. "My folks used to have a summer house here."

"Did they?" The clean-shaven man seemed amused. "Well, that almost makes you a home boy then, don't it?" He pointed to his friend. "That's Polk. I'm Eddie."

"Frank." He offered his hand, but Eddie was already pointing to the men at the grill.

"Over there's Teal and Mace." He shouted: "Teal! Mace! This here's Frank."

The barbecuer waved his hamburger turner, and Frank nodded. "Well," he said to Eddie, "I think I'll go sit—"

"You still got that house, Frank?" Polk asked.

Frank shook his head. "My father sold it a few years ago."

"So who you been visiting?"

"Well, nobody, really."

"So why'd you come back?"

"He told you, Polk," Eddie said. "He came for the fireworks."

"Oh, right."

"Polk's a little slow," Eddie said. "Don't mind him. Have a beer with us, Frank?"

"That's okay. I brought my own."

Eddie frowned. "Something wrong with our hospitality?"

"No, I just—"

"What you got there, anyway, Frank?" Eddie pointed to the paper bag.

"Sandwiches."

"No shit? Let me see." Frank hesitated, then handed him the bag. Eddie pulled out a sandwich. "Chicken." He held it up for Polk to see. "And chicken. Two chicken sandwiches."

"Huh," Polk said.

"Polk, why don't you get our friend here a beer?" Eddie put the sandwiches back, carefully folded the bag, and handed it to Frank, who resigned himself to having a beer with them. Eddie dimly reminded him of somebody from his past, but who? Frank couldn't recall.

Eddie leaned against the Triumph. "You say you used to come up here summers, Frank?"

"We had a house about a few miles off Lake Road. Up from where that Mini-Mart is now."

"That's not the place burned down?"

"No, no."

Polk returned with the beers, accompanied by one of the
men from the grill. "Mace, what's that place burned down off
Lake Road?" Eddie asked the newcomer.

"Brenner place," Mace said.

"Why, I knew them," Frank said. "Mr. Brenner used to
go fishing with my dad. They had a daughter who got killed in
a car crash."

"That's them."

"Their place burned down?"

"About five years ago."

"Jesus."

"Hard-luck family," Eddie said.

"Brenner got into a little fight with some boys down at
the marina about some repair work on his boat," Polk said.
"Place burned down over the winter that year."

"You mean . . . they burned it?" Frank asked.

"No, I don't mean that."

"Things happen sometimes, Frank," Eddie said. "Coinci-
dences. It's spooky. You think there's a connection, but there
ain't none. It's just the way things go."

"Those poor people," Frank said.

"Yeah, they don't come here no more," Polk said.

They were silent for a moment.

"Where you from, Frank?" Mace asked.

"Pittsburgh."

"Hey," Polk said. "One thing Pittsburgh's got that we
don't is niggers. You got a lot of niggers there, don't you?"

"I don't know," Frank said uneasily.

"What—can't see them?" He laughed, and Mace did
too.

"Come on, Polk," Eddie said. "Don't act ignorant." He
winked at Frank. "He don't bother you, does he?"

Frank shook his head.

"Just don't mind him. Some of his best friends are niggers, you know."

"Hell they are," Polk muttered.

Frank took a deep swig of his beer.

"Why're you here, anyway, Frank?" Mace asked.

"Shit," Eddie said. "How many times we gotta hear this? He's here for the fucking fireworks."

"You come all the way up here just to see fireworks?"

"I wanted to look around a bit," Frank said. "My folks used to—"

"I hope we don't have to go through all this again just for you, Mace," Eddie said.

"Well, up yours," Mace said.

Frank finished his beer and crumpled the can. "Well, I guess I'll be taking off."

Eddie looked surprised. "Hey, I thought you were staying for the fireworks."

"Well, I—"

"Polk didn't offend you now, did he?"

"Oh no. No."

"So why're you running off?"

"I'm not. I just—"

"You don't mind our company, do you?"

"No, no."

"Well, hell," Eddie said affably. "Sit awhile. Have another beer."

Frank didn't know what to do.

"Hey, let me see that." Eddie pointed to Frank's cap. "Come on, come on," he urged. Frank handed it to him. Eddie put it on, squared it. "You know," he said to Polk, "I always wanted to have me one of these Yankees caps."

"You're a Yankees fan?" Frank asked.

"Hell, no. I hate that fucking team."

Mace raised his beer. "Pirates all the way."

"I just always wanted to have one," Eddie said. "It's like wearing your enemy's ears or balls or something. The Hottentots or Genghis Khan or somebody used to do that."

"Fucking niggers," Polk snorted.

"Polk," Eddie said patiently, "Genghis Khan wasn't no nigger." He looked at Frank and shook his head, as if to say, *What can you do?* He tipped up the Triumph's side-view mirror and stared into it. "Yankees," he murmured. He seemed absorbed in his reflection. "You married, Frank?"

"No, divorced."

Eddie looked up, his grin quick and knifelike. "I thought so. I could tell that about you. Any kids?"

"No."

"Footloose and fancy-free, huh?"

"Sure. I guess." Eddie's questions made him uncomfortable. He'd get his cap back, then go.

"Hey, Frank." Mace had walked to the rear of the Triumph. "You know you got a Save the Whales bumper sticker back here?"

"Save the whales?" Eddie said.

"Sure enough."

"Fuck the whales," Polk said.

"Hey, come on, Polk," Eddie said. "Whales're beautiful." He winked again at Frank. "It's all right. I can relate."

"I seen one on Atlantic Beach once," Polk said. "Only time I been to the ocean, and there he was. Big sorry motherfucker. Just threw himself up on that beach there. Just wheezing away. Got himself a real big crowd."

"They say they're pretty smart animals," Mace said.

"Well, it was real dumb-ass what that whale did, that's for sure."

"Here's to whales," Eddie said. Except for Frank, who had none, they all raised their beers. "Hey, Frank, you're still empty. You sure you don't want another?"

"No, really, I've got to get going." He waited for Eddie to give him back his cap.

"You know, Frank, I got a sense about you." Eddie tapped the bill of the cap. "Now let me guess. I think you're the kind of guy who had a McGovern bumper sticker a few years back, right?"

"That's right," Frank said. "I did."

"And maybe a—who was it?—a McCarthy sticker before that?"

"Well, no—"

"Or maybe a Get Out of Vietnam sticker, then. Am I right?"

"No," Frank lied. "I didn't."

"You serve in Vietnam, Frank?" Polk asked.

Frank shook his head.

"How come? You weren't a damn hippie now, were you?" Polk's eyes narrowed. He wiped his mouth with the back of his hand.

"I . . . had a deferment."

"What for? Got bad feet or something?"

"No." Frank hesitated. "It was a . . . an occupational deferment."

"What the hell's that?"

"I had a job the draft board thought was in the national interest."

Polk and Eddie exchanged glances.

"Well, what was this job, Frank?" Eddie asked. "That was so important and all?"

"I was—an educator," Frank said.

"A teacher?"

"Well, I . . . I didn't teach, exactly. I worked with a company that made up tests." Frank saw their puzzled expressions. "You know, standardized tests in reading and math and so on. For young kids." They still looked puzzled. "I helped make up test questions."

"They let you out of Vietnam for *that?*" Polk said.

"It wasn't me. It was their decision."

"But you had to ask them for that deferment," Eddie said. "Didn't you?"

Frank was silent.

"Hey, you guys!" Teal shouted from the grill. "Food's on!"

"You weren't scared to go, were you, Frank?" Eddie asked.

"I . . . nobody wanted to go to that war."

"That's not what I asked. I asked, were *you* scared?"

"No, I . . . I . . . of course not."

"Well, you're a brave man, Frank." Eddie raised his beer in another toast. "A better man than me. I sure was scared."

Frank flushed. "You were over there?"

Eddie nodded. "Me and Teal."

"You tell him, Eddie," Polk said. He was smiling.

Eddie counted on his fingers. "Ben Hu, Que Duc, the Delta—one shitty place after another."

"Huh," Frank said.

"You know," Eddie said, "a lot of guys over there didn't much care for the guys who got to stay home. I mean, there you were, getting your ass zinged, eating those shitty peaches, and there was this guy back home, eating a chili dog, screwing your sister—"

"You don't got a sister," Mace said.

"I didn't say this was *me*, Mace. I'm talking about your

guys in general. Now don't worry, Frank. Me—I didn't hate that guy at all. Hell, no. More fucking power to him. He was smarter'n me. He got out."

"He got a deferment," Polk said.

"Why, I even *admired* him," Eddie said. "I'd think about the absolute good times he was having, and I just admired him. He was smarter'n me. I thought, when I get home, I'm going to shake his hand. And Frank—I'd like to do just that." He thrust out his hand. Frank dumbly, automatically, extended his, and Eddie grasped it and pumped once, twice, and let it fall. "There now."

Polk snickered, and Frank reddened.

Eddie glanced again in the side-view mirror. "Hell, look at me, guys." He fingered a clump of long hair, and laughed. "I'm the one who looks like a hippie now. We're getting older but no wiser. Right, Frank?" He tipped Frank's cap back on his head. "You know, I just love this cap."

"Maybe Frank'll give it to you," Polk said.

"Hey, that'd be real nice." Eddie looked at him, and Frank was startled by the challenge in his eyes. They were all looking at him.

"Sure," Frank said. "You can have it."

"Why, that's nice of you, Frank." Eddie grinned broadly. "Hey, Teal!" he shouted. "Frank here gave me his fucking Yankees cap."

"You guys ever gonna come eat?" Teal shouted back.

"C'mon, Frank," Eddie said. "Let's get us something to eat."

"I really should get going," Frank said.

"Oh, come on now." Eddie clapped him on the shoulder, held him. "You're not scared of our cooking, now, are you?" He guided Frank toward the grill. "You gave me this nice cap, now

I've got to give you something. We've got to break bread together, like the old Israelites." Eddie speared a hot dog, put it
on a burned bun, and shoved it into Frank's hand. "We'll eat
and have us another beer and then we'll all watch the fireworks,
right? Now you just get yourself some beans and stuff and come
sit with us." He loaded his own plate and walked back to the
pickup. Polk and Mace fixed their hot dogs and hamburgers and
went over to sit with him on the tailgate.

Frank lingered at the grill. He bit into his hot dog.

Why, why had he given Eddie his cap? It was so stupid.
If they hadn't all been standing around, making him nervous—

"Don't let him get to you," Teal said. "Eddie's okay. He
just likes to needle folks."

Frank hadn't realized he'd overheard. "I don't think he
cares much for me," he said.

Teal flipped over a hamburger. "Eddie don't care much
for nobody. That's Eddie."

"You were in Vietnam together?"

Teal looked puzzled. "What do you mean? Eddie weren't
over there at all. Did he say that?"

"Yes."

Teal snorted and laughed. "That bullshitter. *I* was over
there, but he weren't. He was in the army, but they'd stopped
sending new guys by then."

"But why'd he—"

"He was just bullshitting you."

Frank looked at the three men eating by the truck. Eddie
was saying something to Polk and Mace, and they all laughed.

Just bullshitting me. Frank felt foolish, but also relieved.
They'd just been kidding him. Okay, fine. He'd played the fool,
he'd lost his cap. So what? Let Eddie have it. He'd just go.

The sun had disappeared behind the trees and the sky was

fire-ridden. Frank finished his hot dog. "Well, I better get going," he said.

"Take care," Teal said.

"Hey, Frank," Eddie called as he passed by them. "You're not leaving, are you? The fireworks'll be starting soon."

"No, I've got to go."

"Why? No one's expecting you, are they?"

"I'm a little tired. It's a long drive back."

"Well, it's your deal."

And I'm gone, Frank thought. He'd drive over to the beach and watch the fireworks with everyone else. He wanted to be with a lot of people again, crowds.

"Hey, Frank." Eddie jumped off the tailgate and walked over. "Look, before you go, I was wondering . . . I got a favor to ask." He seemed hesitant, almost shy. "Could I, you know, take your car for a little spin? Just down the road aways?"

"I wouldn't let him do that," Mace yelled.

"I can't," Frank said.

Eddie seemed surprised. "Why not?"

"I . . ." Frank searched for a reason. "My insurance."

"Oh, fuck that," Eddie said. "Come on. It's just gonna be a quick spin."

"No, really, I can't."

"You surely don't think something's gonna happen on this little old road, do you?"

"No, I—"

"Well, what're you scared of, then?"

"I'm not scared. It's just—"

Eddie's brow furrowed. "You don't have something against *me* driving your car, do you?"

"No, no . . ."

Eddie spread his hands. "Well?"

Frank didn't know what to say or do. He couldn't argue with Eddie, and he couldn't just get in his car and go. Again, they were all looking at him.

"Come on, now," Eddie said softly, so that only Frank could hear. "I told Polk and Mace you'd probably let me, cause you're a good guy." He grinned.

"Okay," Frank said. "Just a short ride."

"Hey, Polk," Eddie yelled. "Frank here says we can take his car for a spin."

"Whooee!"

"You're a brave man, mister," Mace called out.

Frank handed him the keys, and Eddie and Polk got in. Eddie revved the engine. Pine needles scattered under the exhaust. He jammed the gear stick forward and the Triumph lurched toward the lake, barely missing Frank's leg.

"Whooee!" Polk yelled.

Ten yards from the bank, Eddie braked, glanced back, and ground the car into reverse. Kicking up pine needles and dust, it shot up the slope straight toward a tree stump—*he'll see it,* Frank thought, *he'll swerve*—but Eddie didn't, and the Triumph slammed dully into it.

Frank ran over. Eddie and Polk were already out, inspecting the damage. The rear bumper was dented like a piece of bad fruit.

"Sorry about this." Eddie shook his head. "I don't know where that damn stump *came* from."

"You saw it!" Frank cried. "Jesus—"

"Sure didn't."

"You rammed it on purpose!"

"Hey, now." Eddie held up his hand.

"Did you see?" Frank appealed to Mace and Teal, who had just arrived.

"Wasn't watching," Mace said. Teal shook his head.

"It's no big thing," Polk said. "Car'll still run."

"Dammit, why'd you do it?"

"I told you," Eddie said. "It just happened."

"It's just a little bump," Polk said. "You can get a hammer and pound that right out."

"Frank, look here." Eddie pulled two five-dollar bills from his wallet. "Here's ten dollars. That oughta be plenty for getting it pounded out."

"You can't just pound it out!" Frank ran his fingers along the dent. "They're going to have to replace the whole damn bumper."

"Here's my ten dollars."

"Look at this." Frank gestured helplessly.

"Real, real sorry."

"Who's your insurance company?"

"Oh, come on, Frank." Eddie looked disgusted. "We don't want to bother them now, do we? With this little old thing?"

"Somebody's got to pay for this!"

Eddie waved the bills.

"Who's your insurance company?" Frank asked again.

Eddie sighed. "You know, I don't really recall offhand, Frank. It's back there with my papers."

"You can call your agent."

"Don't remember him, either."

"Hey, mister," Polk said. "Are you a fucking lawyer or something?"

Eddie rocked slightly on the balls of his feet. He and Frank stared at one another.

"You know who your agent is, don't you?" Frank said.

Eddie's eyes narrowed. "You calling me a liar now too, Frank?"

"Look, I just—"

"Are you?" Eddie's voice rose.

"Look, friend," Mace said reasonably, "why don't you just take the man's money and go? No trouble. Nothing to get excited about."

"He don't want my ten dollars, Mace," Eddie said. He put the bills in his pocket. "My money's not good enough for him."

"He sure does bitch and moan a lot," Polk said.

"Don't he, though," Eddie said.

"All about a little dent."

"Look," Frank said. "You smashed my bumper. You—"

"I'm getting real tired of you accusing me of things, Frank," Eddie said angrily. "You know that? Maybe you'd best just get out of here."

Frank looked desperately to Teal. Almost imperceptibly, Teal shook his head.

"Go on," Eddie said. He came toward Frank. "Get the hell out of here."

Frank moved back to the car door.

"Get!" Eddie hissed.

Frank opened the door. "I'll call the police," he said, his voice cracking slightly.

"You do that," Eddie said. "Go cry to them."

Frank started to get in. "I need the keys," he said.

Eddie reached into his shirt pocket and threw the keys on the ground between them. His face burning, Frank walked over, stooped down, and picked them up. Someone snickered. His ears were ringing, and Frank wasn't even aware of driving until he was through the pines, almost to the beach, and then the ringing lessened and he felt only humiliation and the acid taste of shame. He stopped at the end of the road across from the Mini-Mart.

"Bastards!" He hit his palm against the steering wheel. "Goddam bastards."

He got out and looked at the dented bumper.

"Ten dollars," he muttered. "Ten fucking dollars."

Frank crossed the road to the outdoor phone. He was agitated and couldn't decide whether to call the highway patrol or the local police, and when he decided on the police, couldn't remember the name of the community he was in. All the times he'd come here, and he couldn't remember. He found a police emergency number in the front of the directory, started to dial, then hesitated. Even if he could get a cop out here on a Fourth of July evening for a dented bumper, wouldn't Eddie and the others be long gone by the time he arrived? And if they weren't, wouldn't they all stick up for Eddie anyway?

He sure does bitch and moan a lot, Polk had said. He could see them all looking at him with contempt: he'd gone and cried to the police, after all.

He hung up. *Just go,* he told himself. *Forget it, just get out of here.*

Frank recrossed the road and got back in the car. He turned on the engine, but didn't pull away. Instead he stared out the windshield.

They humiliated me, he thought. *And I let them.* His face burned as he remembered.

But what else could he have done? He'd been outnumbered, Eddie was crazy, the fender, after all, wasn't that big a deal. And besides—

You weren't scared, were you? Eddie had asked. And suddenly Frank knew who Eddie reminded him of, all the way back through the years to Tyler and his youth—Ira Dunn. Frank saw him again, as he'd looked in the mirror over the mantel in Frank's house, when Ira had seemed to stare so deeply into his soul, challenging him, just before he threw the bottle into the TV set and all the world changed.

Frank turned off the engine.

I was scared of him, he thought.

When he'd helped Ira ravage his parents' house, he'd been scared. When he'd run from Polk and Eddie, he'd been scared. When he'd let Eddie drive the car, when he'd given him the cap, he'd been scared.

He was scared now.

I got a sense about you, Eddie had said. He was grinning at him. And behind him was Polk, and behind Polk, Mace and Teal. And behind them, Ira, and others, others—a man on a path on a Cretan mountainside, another drinking *raki* among the Minoan tombs. And still others, those he had lived with and thought he'd loved, his father and mother and Jena, and those he would never know, the children he'd never had, that he'd never wanted—he'd been scared of them all, had run from them just as surely as he was running now.

"I've always been scared," Frank murmured.

He closed his eyes in shame and sorrow, and when he opened them, everyone was gone except for Eddie, Frank's cap perched mockingly on his head.

Frank started the car and turned back toward the pines.

They were sitting at the picnic table now, passing a joint. Polk raised his arm in a half-wave, as if Frank had just gone out for some beer. He parked beside Eddie's truck and walked toward them. They sat in silence, like kings in judgment.

"I want my cap back," he said to Eddie.

Eddie took a deep hit off the joint, held the smoke, then expelled it harshly. "I thought you gave me this cap, Frank."

"He did, Eddie," Polk said.

"I didn't mean to," Frank said.

"Here, have a hit." Eddie offered him the joint. Frank shook his head. Eddie shrugged and passed it to Mace.

"I'd just like it back," Frank said. His heart was pounding—he was sure they could hear.

Eddie sighed. "That sort of makes you like an Indian giver, don't it?"

"He's still hot about the car, Eddie," Polk said.

"I don't care about the car."

Eddie folded his arms. "Why do you want that hat now, Frank?"

"I . . . it's mine. I didn't mean to give it away."

Eddie pursed his lips. In the deepening twilight, his face was a mask. "How much you want it, Frank?" He pulled the cap lower on his head. Polk laughed sharply.

"You want to fight," Frank said. "That's what you want, isn't it?"

"Hey now," Mace said.

"Nobody said nothing about fighting." Eddie took the cap off and twirled it on his finger.

"Oh, give him the damn hat, Eddie," Teal said. "Quit dicking around."

Eddie carefully put it back on. Frank flushed. As if they were the words of a stranger, he heard himself saying, "Okay, I'll fight you! If that's what you want, I'll fight you."

"You really want to fight for it, Frank?" Eddie seemed amused. "This little old hat?" He slowly rose, crossed in front of the table, and stood not more then ten yards away.

"Watch out now," Polk said.

"Eddie—" Teal said.

"Well, Frank wants to fight, Teal." Eddie looked at him. "Don't you?"

Frank felt a lightness in his stomach, as if he were falling.

He didn't know what to do. He knew nothing about fighting.

Eddie spread his arms. "Don't you?"

Frank swallowed. "What—what are the rules?"

Polk groaned. "I told you he was a lawyer, Eddie."

Eddie reached into his jeans and pulled out a knife. "Hey, these are the rules, Frank." The blade snicked open.

"Eddie—" Teal said, and Mace whistled softly.

Absurdly, Frank said, "That's not fair."

"That's right. It's not. It's just the way things go."

"Eddie, put that damn thing away," Teal ordered. He rose from the table, but made no further move.

"Hey," Frank said. "Come on."

"Come on where, Frank?" Eddie poked the air between them. "Where do you want to go now?"

"This . . . this is crazy!"

"Oh, I *am* crazy." He began circling Frank. "I'm the craziest thing you've ever dreamed of."

"Eddie," Teal said, "quit fucking *around*."

Farther down the lake, a string of firecrackers pop-popped. Frank heard shouts and laughter, impossibly far away. In all the world, he was alone.

"These're Vietnam jungle rules, Frank," Eddie said, brandishing the knife. "See now? See what you missed?"

"You better take off, mister," Mace said.

Eddie circled, yet came no closer. And Frank realized that Eddie was going to let him run, that he could if he wanted to—he would be allowed that final humiliation. It was, after all, only what was expected of him.

"You didn't go to Vietnam!" Frank cried.

Eddie cocked his head. "How's that, Frank?"

"You didn't go to Vietnam either. I know you!"

Eddie stared at him, knife at arm's length. He glanced back at the table.

"You didn't, Eddie," Teal said.

Eddie grinned. "Well, you sure can't put one over on old Frank, can you?"

"He's a lawyer, Eddie," Polk said.

Something searing, neither rage nor shame but of them both, passed through him then, and Frank yelled, "I'm not a lawyer, goddam you! You don't know a goddam thing about me!" He shook his fists at Eddie. "I'll fight you! Goddammit, if that's you want, I'll *fight* you."

"Don't be a fool, mister," Mace said. "Take off."

"No, goddammit!"

Eddie stood motionless, the knife extended, his smile frozen tight. "Don't be crazy," he said.

"I don't *care*," Frank cried. "Come on!"

Eddie squinted, as if trying to see him better in the fading light. The knife blade wavered slightly.

"Come on," Frank said. "You've got the knife, come *on*."

Eddie didn't move.

"Goddam you!" Frank cried. "All your goddam talk . . ." He took a step toward Eddie.

"You're crazy, man." Eddie folded the knife and put it in his pocket. He spread his hands and grinned. "I can't fight anybody crazier than me."

He took off the Yankees cap and tossed it at Frank's feet. For a moment, Frank couldn't move, couldn't stop watching him. Slowly he unclenched his fists. He picked up the cap and turned it over.

"Happy now?" Eddie said.

Frank put it on.

"Maybe you'd best go now," Teal said.

"I'm not going anywhere." Frank heard his voice come from far away. "I'm going to watch the fireworks." He walked past them, down the slope to the lake.

Frank sat on the dock's edge: it was dark now, and the lake smelled deep and mossy. His hands shook, lightly at first, then harder, and he hugged himself, as if that might contain the shaking. A first rocket flared and fell, followed by another that opened like a rose. "I won," he said softly.

Frank looked across the lake to the summer house and, yes, in the rocket's light, imagined he could see it, bright and warm and open. They were all there—his mother and father and Jena, waiting to receive him, to bind his wounds. They opened the door to greet him, Jena and his mother smiling, touching his arm, while his father, eyes glistening, stood shyly apart and nodded approvingly. *He had always been afraid, too,* Frank realized with wonder. How stupid, he thought, never to have understood this about his father until now. Frank felt like crying for him, and indeed for them all, crying in sorrow and in shame, for their pain and his ignorance. "I'm not going anywhere," he told them, taking them to himself. "I'm staying right here."

The rocket faded; they were gone. He had won, but there was no one left to tell, nor to weep with, nor to care.

Three more rockets, red and white and yellow, burst over the lake. In their light, Frank saw Teal and Polk and Mace and Eddie, faces turned skyward, almost reverent. They were who remained for him, the only ones left to hear.

"I'm not going anywhere!" he shouted, but they gave no sign of having heard. The rockets faded, they disappeared, and he was alone once more. "I'm not going anywhere," he murmured. "I'm not going anywhere at all."

In the Night

—August 1990

In *the night,* the dead of night, close and insistent and whining, the phone is ringing. My eyes blink, snap open. Yellow streetlights cast tree-shadows from the park onto the ceiling of my apartment. It's August, hot, and I've been sleeping without a sheet. I grope for the receiver—a call in the night is almost always a bad business, a death, a crank, at best a wrong number, voices from the night to shake your sleep or snare your soul—and I mumble, "Hello?"

I hear a soft exhalation of breath, although it might be line noise, and I wonder if anyone is there, maybe I only dreamed the phone was ringing, but then she says, "Oh, Frank, oh God, I'm so *glad* you're there! I woke you, I'm sorry, I know I did, but I'm just so glad you're there." It's Allie, the woman I've been seeing. I glance at the clock, its blue digital numerals cool and reassuring—2:46. Before I can say anything, she's talking again, and I hear the distress in her voice. "Frank, I was so scared you weren't home. I know you're a heavy sleeper, but the phone kept ringing and ringing, and I didn't—"

"Where are you, Allie?" I ask, even though I know. She's at her sister's in Punxalawtie, state forest country—she's gone up there this weekend to visit. Sandy's husband, a doctor, has just walked away from his practice, their two children, and her. According to Allie, he told Sandy he needed some spiritual renewal. As if you could just run out and buy it at the grocery store.

"Frank, I'm so frightened."

"What's wrong, Allie? What's happened?" She's called me before in the night, that's not unusual: Allie thinks it's sexy to talk with your lover across the soft dark milk of night when you're both in bed. And sometimes she calls because she's had one of her frequent nightmares, and I listen to dreams in which she's twisted and pulled apart by silent, open-mouthed people, or is abandoned in great houses with rooms that empty, door upon door, onto barred balconies, catwalks to nowhere. Her voice becomes small and wounded when she tells me these dreams. But this is different—something's really wrong. She's breathing heavily, almost crying.

I reach to turn on the bedside lamp, then decide not to. The dark is better to talk in.

I met Allie a few months ago at the Daily Bread bakery, where I often stopped for coffee and an oatmeal-raisin cookie after riding my bike, something I'd taken up to get in better shape. Allie had just started working there. She asked me if I felt like a kid on my red bike, and I asked why, and she said she'd always thought red was the color of childhood. Her voice had a catch to it, as if she weren't quite certain how I'd react to this.

I laughed. "Now I'll feel like a kid," I told her. "I should get a playing card and clip it on the spokes—you know, to make a motor sound?" She laughed at that.

Later she told me I'd looked really sexy in my shorts and tank top. I was surprised: first, because I hadn't even realized she'd been looking, and second, because sexy was one thing I hadn't considered myself for a long time. After all, I was a middle-aged man with worry lines in his forehead and a slight roll to the waist. Allie was in her early thirties, tall and thin, brown hair cut short, almost carelessly choppy. Her eyes—what I noticed first—were deep green and wide as the sea. They'd grow wider when she talked with you, wider still when she listened. They gave her face a haunted look, as if a dark fire had once burned through it, leaving it ghostly and hollow, except for those eyes.

I ordered some Irish soda bread. As Allie cut it, I noticed her fingernails, which were picked almost to the quick, the skin around the cuticles sore from fresh abrasions. To my surprise, I found myself wanting to hold those hands. I wanted to kiss them, and more—I wanted to heal them. I wanted to make love to that haunted look, to fill it, to bring it peace.

Allie's not always been well: there have been times "away," as she puts it, in rest homes and hospitals, some voluntary, some not. After the last one, she'd stayed with Sandy and her husband for a time before mustering the courage to come to Pittsburgh. Her parents, both dead now, left her a small trust. Between that and a series of part-time jobs—clerking in a bookstore, refinishing furniture in a secondhand furniture shop, the bakery—she makes ends meet. She told me once she knew her life was never going to amount to very much, and I protested, saying, "How can you say that?" But she just nodded her head, and said she'd stopped fighting it, it was just the way things go.

And I told her, no, you can always make things different. She asked me if I really believed that, or if I was just saying that because I *wanted* to believe it or because I thought maybe it would make her feel better—two wrong reasons right there—and I thought for a moment, then told her I really wanted to believe it, and maybe that was just as good anyway.

"I'm so scared, Frank," she says again, now, in the night. "I was driving and it—it was dark *everywhere,* I didn't realize it would be so dark, no cars, no lights—"

"Allie, where *are* you? Aren't you at Sandy's?"

"No. I left Sandy's about an hour ago. I don't know where I am, and—" She catches her breath. "No. I'm at a phone booth somewhere. It's in the middle of nowhere. Frank, it's so *dark.*"

"You left Sandy's? At two in the morning?"

"I just got so restless, Frank. Sandy's so depressed, and the kids are just miserable and snotty. And Sandy"—her voice quavers—"she's been blaming *me* for what happened with Alex. She said if I hadn't lived with them so long, putting a strain on their marriage—oh God, Frank, it was horrible, I had to get out of there—"

"Allie, where *are* you?"

"I don't *know!* Somewhere between Punxalawtie and Clarion. I j-just got on the road back at Sandy's and followed a sign to Clarion, because I knew I had to go there before I could get Route 80 back to Pittsburgh. That's right, isn't it, Frank? Clarion to Route 80? But I haven't seen a sign *since.*"

"Where's this phone booth, Allie?"

"At a gas station—just an old country gas station. It's closed, Frank. There's a sign for a . . . a turkey shoot on the door. One of the windows is boarded over. Frank"—her voice is taut, she's trying to control herself—"there's no moon, no stars, nothing. There's no bulb in the phone booth even. It's just so *dark.*

Just woods all around, all down the road. I was driving along, and
I got so scared. I haven't seen one single car since—no, that's
wrong—there was *one*, it crept up behind me about five miles
out of Punxalawtie, I thought it was one of those guys who creep
real close to you and won't let you go, but then it passed, just
shot right ahead and away, and I haven't seen anybody since.
I—"

"Allie, easy—"

"And there're no *signs!* Shouldn't there be signs? The
one back at Punxalawtie said Clarion was thirty miles, but I
know I've driven longer than that, Frank, I know I'm lost—"

"You haven't seen *any* signs? No route signs even?"

"There's nothing, Frank. No signs, no stores, no houses.
Just hills. Trees."

I feel helpless. I can't drive up to find Allie, since I no
longer have a car—I sold the TR-3 in an effort to simplify my
life—and even if I did, could I really expect Allie, in her state,
to wait in a phone booth in the dark for three hours until I could,
maybe, find her somewhere on the road between Punxalawtie
and Clarion?

"Allie, look. Do you want me to call the state police? I
can have them look for—"

"No!" Her cry is sharp, pained. "Don't do that!"

"Why not, Allie? They'd—"

"They'd think I was so . . . so—*helpless.* I—I couldn't
bear that."

"Allie, they—"

"They'll take me away." She says it tersely, but I feel she's
ready to burst into tears. "They'll think I can't—I can't *bear*
things again, and—no. No. No."

I look out my window. All the streetlights are on except
for one at the very end, its lamp burned out. I gaze up the street,

as if I could see all the way north to Allie, somewhere in the night. "Tell me what happened, Allie," I say. "Tell me exactly."

"I was driving along," she says, "and everything was closing in, getting darker. I thought my lights were going out, and I kept flicking them from high to low to high, and they were working, but everything was still getting dimmer. And I b-began to think maybe I . . . I was going blind or something, and I'd run off the road, and be killed—"

"Allie—"

"It's all thick woods here, Frank. And hills. You could run off the road and they'd never find you—"

"Allie, you're not going to run off the road. You're not going blind."

"—and I started thinking, maybe they're out there, waiting for me, maybe they *want* me to die—"

"Who, Allie?"

"*Everybody,* Frank. The dead. My father and mother, my grandmother, my cousin Doris who drowned, the little boy across the street who got killed when his mother backed up the car over him—everybody. I was driving along, and I could remember them all. They're waiting for me, Frank. I can *feel* them out there."

"Allie—"

"They want me dead, too." I hear the panic in her voice. "I—I wanted to stop, but there was nowhere to stop, it was all just road and darkness, and then I saw this gas station and the phone—"

"Allie, Allie, calm down. It's all your imagination. They're not out there at all."

She sighs, a bone-hard, dead-down sigh, as if her spirit would leave her body. "But what if they *are* there, Frank? The dead?"

"Allie, come on."

"I mean, if there's a God, why couldn't they be? If there's a God, then He must take souls to Him—or something like that. Wouldn't He? So they're alive *somewhere.* Why couldn't they be here?"

"The dead are dead, Allie."

"But they *can't* be, Frank! Not if there's a God!"

"They just want to rest, then. They don't want us dead, too." I don't really know what I'm saying, I'm just talking, trying to calm her. "I don't think they want to bother with us anymore at all."

She's quiet, and I listen to the breeze stirring the trees in the park, the crickets in the grass. All my life I've heard them chirp and never wondered why they do it. Are they calling to one another? Or just making sounds to pass away the night? I feel I should know.

"We don't have any bodies," she says.

"What?"

"Right now you're just a voice, and I'm just a voice. No bodies. Like ghosts."

"Sure." I laugh.

"Ghosts."

"Ghosts don't carry on conversations, Allie. Only people do."

She's silent again, as if considering that. She sighs. "I'm tired, Frank. I never should have left Sandy's."

"Allie, listen. Get in the car. Turn on the overhead light. Turn on the radio. Just drive slowly. You can make it to Clarion. There'll be a gas station, a 7-Eleven, something open there. And there's a motel, the . . . the . . ." I think hard: I'd stayed there once with Jena. "The Starliter. You can get a room. You can drive back to Pittsburgh tomorrow."

"What if I can't?" She says it so softly I almost don't hear.

"Can't what?"

"Can't make it to Clarion? What if I just start screaming and screaming—I'm so afraid I'll scream—and there's no phone this time?"

"Allie, you can make it. Believe me."

"But what if I *can't?* You don't . . . you don't know what—what it's like—"

"What, Allie?"

"To just not *know.* You get up in the morning, Frank, and you *know* what's going to happen. You're going to have breakfast and buy your newspaper and go to work, and you *know* you'll get there, and people will be there. You'll talk to them, and they'll talk to you, and you'll understand each other. You can count on it. You can *count* on things, Frank. And you never even think about it. You just expect it. It's your due. Like a king."

I know I should say something, but it's like the night has swallowed me, too, and my words, and my thoughts. She's taunting me, I think. *See?* she's saying. *See how little you really know?* And I'm angry that I can't say anything that will make a difference. My hand tightens around the receiver. I want to hang up the phone hard. *Go away,* I want to tell her, *leave me alone, let me sleep. Let me sleep a hundred years.* And then I realize I'm more than angry. I'm scared, too. Whether she wanted to or not, she's scared me. *Maybe they* are *out there,* I think. It all starts to seem real, the night an endless waste of the dead, waiting for us to join them. Maybe Allie is only one among them.

I stare into the night and it seems to open before me to yet another night, winter, I'm standing on a frozen lake, the stars obliterated from my sky just as they are from Allie's. I am cold, my nose is running. The ice is groaning under and around me so loud, it seems my ears will crack, and I am scared. I am a boy, no more than nine or ten. I am waiting for something—a voice, a sign, courage . . .

"Frank?" Allie's voice is small and faraway. "Are you there?"

I know what that boy is doing. And suddenly I do have something to say to Allie.

"It's the strangest thing," I tell her. "I was just remembering how when we were kids we used to go skating on the lake in Tyler. Where I grew up."

"Skating?"

"Yep. It was always a little dangerous skating there because there were all these different thicknesses of ice. Lake currents did that. You had to be careful, because all of a sudden you could be on a real thin patch, and then—*kablooie!* Right down under. Most of the time you could tell things by the color—blue or white ice was okay, but shades of gray, that was bad. Black was the worst, because that meant the ice was so thin you could see the water right below."

"It . . . sounds scary."

"Sometimes we used to go skating at night, Allie. We weren't supposed to, but we'd go anyway. That was really scary. You couldn't tell colors anymore at all. You could be coming on a real thin patch and never know."

"Huh."

"We were crazy kids! Listen. We used to *dare* each other to skate out where you didn't know what the ice was like, away from the safe areas we knew. Out there in the strange parts of the lake, in the dark—now *that* was scary!"

She's listening, I know. And I tell her more: I describe the night, the stars like raindrops, or maybe none at all if clouds had covered them, the squeals and shouts and laughter of the other skaters getting fainter and fainter as you skated farther out onto the ice and into the night, until finally all you could hear was the snick and skirr of your blades, the only sound beside your sniffling and chuffing. I tell her how it felt—the freedom and the fear of it, knowing any moment the ice could crack and break like a dry bone. "Sometimes you could almost feel the ice *sinking* as you went over, like a bad mattress," I tell her, and I hear her take in a breath. "And your stomach would just . . . *flip* a little, you know? Like on a roller coaster."

"You must have been crazy little kids," she says.

"Oh, we were. We were crazy."

"Did you . . . ever fall in?"

"No. Because there was a secret. That's what I'm getting to."

"A secret? What?"

"The secret was it didn't *matter* if the ice was too thin. If you just skated fast enough, you could glide right over the thin spots. You'd be gone before the ice even felt you were there. And you'd make it."

She's silent. And then: "If you just went fast enough?"

"Yes. And kept moving."

"That's *all?* That was it?"

"That's it."

"I don't believe you."

"It's true, Allie. Look—I'm here to tell you."

She's quiet for a long moment.

"And have faith," I say.

"Faith," she murmurs.

"Or at least don't think about it."

My face is tingling, as if I'd really been out there in the cold. I don't hear Allie's breathing anymore, and for a moment,

I'm afraid she's gone, slipped through the night, but then she says softly, "Okay."

"You'll come to another phone booth somewhere, Allie. You call me again from there. Call me from every phone booth between there and Clarion. When you get to Clarion, get a room at the Starliter. Don't worry about waking anybody up. And then call me from there."

"Okay," she says.

"You'll be all right?"

"The Starliter?"

"Yes. Call me when you get there."

She doesn't reply for a while, then says, "Maybe you were just lucky, Frank. Skating like that. Did you ever think of that?"

"If God can allow ghosts," I tell her, "He can allow a stupid kid a little luck."

The shadows seem to have settled on the ceiling and wall. Outside, the crickets have stopped chirping. It seems the whole night is listening.

"Okay," she says, a sigh more than anything. And before I can say anything else, she's hung up. I lie back on the pillow and pull up the sheet. Despite the night's mugginess, I feel chill.

It was all a lie, of course. There was no lake in Tyler, only a small, sad pond, no bigger than the county swimming pool really, and I doubt that the water there was more than three feet deep, maximum. I never even skated there much—I was never one for winter sports, not like Jena. It had all been a lie, some strange mix of that long-ago winter night with Jena on the lake and this night here with Allie. A lie. A story. Yet somehow, as I was talking, it felt real, as if it *had* happened, as if fantasy and fear could become memory, just by imagining strongly enough, and by telling it to someone. If it wasn't true, still, it was true enough, and truer than most things I'd said in my life.

And the strangest thing: suddenly my life seemed different, more redeemable somehow, if only because any of it could become a story to tell, to help someone in the night. It was my life beyond itself. It was my life better than myself. It was, I thought, what love might be.

Lying back against the coolness of the pillows, waiting for Allie's next phone call, I thought about it all. And in the morning, when she was finally asleep and I awoke from the night, I knew I would still remember, and think about it some more.

About the Author

David Michael Kaplan is the author of *Comfort*, a collection of
stories (Viking Penguin). His fiction has appeared in *The
Atlantic, Redbook, Playboy, Triquarterly, The Ohio Review,* and
other magazines, and has been anthologized in *Best American
Short Stories* and *O. Henry Prize Stories.* Four of Kaplan's
stories have appeared in the PEN Syndicated Fiction Project
Series. He teaches at Loyola University in Chicago, where he
lives.